DEADLY ALLEGIANCE

K.G.H ROBINSON

ISBN: 978-1-960764-41-6 (sc)
ISBN: 978-1-968537-15-9 (hc)
ISBN: 978-1-960764-42-3 (eBook)

www.writeandreleasepublishing.com

For the ones who need a little push,
You are capable of more than you think.

Ignorant Rejection

Burn it down.

Watch as the windows shatter.

Relish the heat on your face and the smoky flavor in the air.

The crackling of the fire as it danced against the wood was music to the ears.

Burning it all down—what a satisfying end to the story.

But hey, that saying, "Don't fight fire with fire," carries a valuable lesson. But whoever said it probably didn't have much at stake nor did they have an arsonist in their back pocket.

Don't fight fire with fire.

But it's not really fighting when the jackass who started it ends up roasting in the flames. All you need is a killer instinct and a few million dollars, and then your fire will be the biggest.

The only one causing damage.

But that's what he gets.

You shouldn't start a fight with someone born to fight. You might just end up burned.

Someone should have warned the guy.

Poor fellow.

Now, the powerful Mr. Crane has been reduced to nothing but a tiny pile of ash.

Serves him right.

Don't fight fire with fire!

Don't take on an ex-assassin with amateurs!

Don't challenge someone stronger than you!

Just don't start a fight.

And always remember to read the fine print!

DON'T FUCK WITH SEAN BARNES!

I'll burn your work to the ground.

And I'll enjoy every second of watching it turn to ash.

AUGUST 15ᵀᴴ, 2163

"Again!"
The wall caved in where my fist met it.
"Again!"
The hole deepened, and cracks grew around the edge.
"Again!"
"Again!"
"AGAIN!"
The wall crumbled around the cracks. Finally, the other side of the room was visible through the fist-sized hole.
"That's how it should have been with your first punch!"
"Again!"
My fist slammed into the surface once more.
Crack!
But this time, the impact was different. Softer. Too soft. The resistance gave way too easily. And suddenly wet. Something sharp pressed against my forearm, and an odd, gurgling sound echoed from the wall.

A droplet of thick liquid dripped onto my inner elbow, its warmth spreading uncomfortably against my skin. Instinct took over and I quickly pulled my arm back.

Thud

That was weird. No criticism? There was always criticism.
At least now I could wipe the sticky liquid off my arm.
But—
Why was it that color?
Why was my arm so red?

Wait... was that blood?

Why would there be blood in the wall?

Did they— did they put someone inside the concrete?

Huh?

Where did the wall go?!

I thought I was in the old training arena.

No

No

No, no, no, no.

NO!

I shouldn't be back here.

I couldn't be back here.

This couldn't be happening.

I can't let this happen. Not again!

But I didn't stop it.

Not this time, nor the first time. And there she was. Choking on her own blood as it filled her throat.

It's strange. The human body works in mysterious ways. You'd think after getting a hole punched through your sternum, would kill someone quickly, especially from blood loss. Not this woman. She clung to life.

I never even learned her name. She was just an assignment. Why would I bother?

But I should have learned her name.

I mean, after all, I was the one who took her life. The one who had to watch the light drain from her eyes. The one who had to confirm her death.

I had to watch as her coffee-like eyes stared deep into mine, as she gurgled on her blood, gasping for air. I don't know if she was trying to speak or breathe. I never knew which one it was. Probably the latter because what could she have said to me?

"I understand"?

"I forgive you"?

"I'm sorry for how this will haunt you forever?"

No. Of course not. She was trying to breathe. That was the only thing that mattered to her at that moment.

Or maybe she was trying to tell me to burn in hell. I would have deserved that. Because I killed her.

And I could have stopped it.

I should have stopped it.

I could have refused the assignment.

But I didn't.

I agreed to the assignment. Her blood was on my hands. Spilled across my soul. A stain I could never wash off, no matter how hard I tried.

I killed her.

Why?

Because if I didn't, someone else would have done it?

She was a wanted woman - desperately wanted dead. Her enemies paid a lot for her death.

Money.

That's why I did it. That's why any of us did it.

Yeah, we were left mentally and emotionally traumatized for life afterward, but at least the paycheck was great. Great enough to cover therapy when we eventually could get the time.

That's a joke.

We weren't even allowed the decency to talk to a professional about our experiences. We were machines. Tools. Why would machines need therapy?

Feelings? Emotions? Ha! No chance.

If we were truly emotionless – I wouldn't be stuck in this reality. I killed a woman because her boyfriend's wife had a lot of money. I had blood on my hands because people paid me to do their dirty work. I was covered in it because the government didn't trust us. I was traumatized because I was built differently than everyone else.

I was a killer because that's what they made me.

Because that's what I had to be.

Yeah, that's the last time I took melatonin to sleep.

I preferred my alternative method - vodka until I passed out. Normally, it took the whole bottle to get me into a calm state. And another half bottle to knock me the fuck out.

Not the safest plan, considering I was always on the edge of alcohol poisoning and choking on my vomit. I couldn't sleep on my side.

Never could. Too vulnerable.

But anyway, there were perks to the alcohol. Either I end up dying, or I sleep with no nightmares. Not that I would really call my passed-out state "sleeping". More like unconsciousness, but at least it kept the nightmares away.

I couldn't deal with the nightmares.

Maybe I should finally get her name. I'm sure someone had to have records of her.

What was I doing again?

Right. The melatonin. I need to get rid of them. I can't be tempted to use them again. I can't deal with the nightmares.

No more nightmares.

But at least this time it was just her. None of the others made an appearance. They didn't come.

In some ways, I should be thankful it was only her.

She wasn't my first assignment, nor will she be my last.

Killing her was simply how I got my paycheck.

At least, she didn't die like how any of the others did. Her death was easy – less torturous.

The wife wanted it done quickly. At least she had some humanity in her, well for the most part. She wasn't like the other clients. The ones who specifically asked for me – my technique – who'd pay extra for the most infliction of pain. And they always wanted proof. Proof that their victim – my victim – had suffered before I finally put an end to their life.

People – sorry –RICH people were twisted and always hungry for more power than their neighbors. So when the government eagerly launched our program, it was no surprise that the spoiled elite found a way to exploit us. We were just tools for them. Machines. Something they could throw money at to handle their dirty work.

Shit!

What time was it?

I had a meeting. I couldn't just sit on my ass all day, replaying that haunting dream.

Get up, lazy ass!

You have a job to do!

Even after all these years away from the original training facility—with its doctors, scientists, and investors—their voices still echoed in my head.

I guess, in the end, they really had programmed me like a machine.

"C'mon, get up, Sean."

I had shit to do before this stupid meeting.

The job was some security gig. Or a bodyguard thing. Who the hell knew? I only applied because I had the most qualifications for jobs like that. It was either this job or some fitness trainer at a gym across the city.

Not that I needed to work. I had enough money to let my great-grandchildren retire at an early age—if I ever had kids. Not that I wanted to have children.

I couldn't risk it.

I can't have them be like me.

Even with the program shut down, there was no guarantee it would stay that way. The company had power—more than anyone realized. And the future? It was never as secure as people liked to believe.

No way in hell was I taking that chance.

Always wrap it before I tap it, or that's what Grandpa Spencer used to say. "Back in my earlier years, this is what all the kids said". The 21st century had some weird sayings from what I've been told.

So I couldn't risk it.

Back to this job. I had made a promise to one of my adoptive mothers, who also happened to be my boss, to try the whole normal job thing. It was one of those well-intentioned, sure, why not? kind of promises. That was a while ago, and I forgot that I couldn't survive forever on fluff and alcohol. So, I guess here I was, trying to get a job. Technically, I'd been unemployed for five years now. Not exactly a great look on a résumé. And it's not like I could explain to potential employers why I'd been jobless for so long or where my experience came from. The last eighteen years of my life were where I had built my actual skill set, but I doubted anyone in at the company wanted to hear about that.

Better call Em before heading over. Have her tweak some dates on my résumé, and make it seem like I hadn't been blowing my past five years on getting high and drunk. I'm sure she wouldn't mind. Not like she had anything better to do.

I'll call her on the way.

Shit! I should call her now since I had to leave.

Thank God, it's ringing.

C'mon, Em, answer the damn phone. I don't have all day.

C'mon, what do you have going on? It's not like you are working.

You've reached the voicemail of -
Fuck!

Let's try this again.

Wait! The last time it only rang once.

This may get her attention.

You've reached the voicemail of -
Bitch! You've got to be kidding me!

I'm not stopping until she fucking answers. I'm pissed!

She was ignoring my calls. You've got to be kidding me! Just leave it, don't decline it.

"Seriously!"

Thank fuck, she answered.

"I don't know who the fuck you think you are but screw you for calling three times. Can't take a fucking hint!"

Em's voice was harsh, and she was irritated.

"You talk to your sister with that attitude?"

"Wha- Excuse you?"

That's cute. There's fear in her voice.

"Calm yourself Em! You haven't been compromised."

The silence that followed was deafening. Then, her voice came through, quieter this time. Unsteady.

"Sean?"

"The one and only."

The call ended with a sharp click, followed by the dull hum of the dial tone, leaving me staring at my phone in disbelief. No fucking way.

"Oh, hell no!"

Now she knew who it was, she better fucking answer!

I called again. Once. Twice. This time, she picked up.

"Stop, Sean! Stop calling me!"

Her voice quivered slightly. She sounded frustrated and almost sad. Maybe it was fear?

I clenched my jaw.

"I can't."

"Sean-"

"I need your expertise! Okay? That's all!"

A bitter laugh came through the speaker. Short. Hollow.

"Really? Why would I help you? After all this time!"

"It's an easy job! Then I'll be on my way-"

"You think it's that easy!"

Her voice spiked with anger.

"Em-"

"Don't 'Em' me! We all thought you were dead in some alleyway!"

I sighed. "Well, I'm not."

Her voice cracked. Shit.

"That's not the point! You've been gone for five years! FIVE!! And not even a call to say you're alive!"

I exhaled through my nose, forcing my tone to stay level.

"Well, Bex or Waverly could have easily found me."

"Sean! That's not the fucking point!"

Her breathing was heavier now. Then, she added.

"Waverly may be our adoptive mother, but she does not control you and she would never violate your freedom like that. You should have call on your own accord!"

"Ok-"

"Especially to us! Do you even know how worried Tilly was?"

I hesitated. Tilly?

She was probably upset for a day or maybe two before going back out and restarting her stupid mission again.

That's the thing about us. We can't let things get to us.

Vulnerability

We couldn't afford to have it. Not when the government and anyone with enough power and money had us by the balls.

As Katya taught us – we get one day to accept the loss. Then, we went back to our jobs. And only when the job was over could we mourn and be upset. But let's be honest: once we stepped back into the field after losing a friend, a brother, a sister, or a family member, we never mourned again.

We were numb.

Watching someone die became as normal as breathing. Just another weekday occurrence.

We knew the Grim Reaper well.

We welcomed Death like an old friend.

And the job? The job never stopped.

So how the hell were we supposed to mourn when we never got the chance to stop?

"Memory! Just fucking shut up!"

Thankfully she went quiet and didn't hang up. Not that I would blame her.

"I get you're upset and want to bitch me out. I don't care. I just need your help changing some things on my résumé. Okay?"

Silence.

Okay. This has gone on long enough.

"Memory!"

Her response was instant, snapping back like a whip.

"You told me to shut up!"

Her voice cracked at the edges, frustration bubbling beneath the surface. I let out a sharp breath.

"Grow up! Now help me!"

Another pause. Then, a low mutter, barely more than a breath.

"And I need to grow up."

She must have thought I wouldn't hear that.

"What was that?"

"Nothing! How am I supposed to do this task of yours?"

I exhaled. Finally.

"So, this company takes online résumés-"

"Of course it does! Most companies do."

"But they don't review them until the person has an interview. And… I may have submitted mine while being under the influence of some things."

Silence.

Then, the driest "Not surprising" I had ever heard.

I swear I could see her hazel eyes rolling through the phone.

"I need you to go in and tweak it so that it doesn't look like I've been jobless and wasting my energy on numbing substances for five years."

"You've been jobless for five years! And Mom hasn't come to kick your ass yet? Damn!"

I winced. "She understands why. You don't need the details."

You get into one fight at your last job, and the person you fight goes into a coma for two years. Then, you become the bad guy. It wasn't entirely my fault.

I had just turned twenty and trying to step away from my previous job. It wasn't the kind of job where I could really put my "skills" to good use, and I was getting restless. One application later, and I was hired at a new nightclub – Bouncer Sean.

They really should have seen that coming.

Long story short, some drunk guy was harassing a few women outside the club. No matter how many times they told him to back off, he wouldn't. Typical intoxicated entitlement. Eventually, I stepped in and told him to leave.

He swung first.

I swung back.

Forgot to pull my punch—just slightly.

Maybe I didn't truly forget.

I broke his ribs on impact and sent him flying into the street right into a passing car.

I can still remember the screams of the women who he was originally harassing. There was genuine fear in their voices and eyes when they called the emergency services. Everyone kept a close eye on me. Almost as if I was a predator at the zoo, who only needed to jump so far to achieve freedom and wreak havoc on the witnesses.

I wasn't charged that night, though I think a few people wished I had been. The police, Waverly and our lawyer all said the same thing "You were doing your job and it was self-defense". It didn't feel like self-defense when the nightmares came. Thanks, melatonin. Also, I received nonstop threats and furious calls from the man's family.

And then, of course. Don't forget the girlfriend, Sean! Can't forget her.

A crowd had gathered around me that night, the whispers and accusations cutting deeper than any punch I'd ever taken.

I could still hear their voices, sharp and relentless, echoing in my mind:

"He would never do such a thing!"
"He's a good guy!"
"He's faithful to me!"
"You've ruined his life! He had a scholarship!"
"I wish he put you in the hospital instead."

I didn't flinch. I understood where they were coming from. Unfortunately. I was somewhat of a monster. Something ripped straight from one of those old—"classic," as Grandpa Spencer would call them—gothic horror novels. There were even some family members who would swear on their lives that the monsters in those stories had once been real.

Totally.

Anyway, I moved after that incident and got fired. "Can't hurt patrons," they said before kicking me out. Not that I fought them on it. I haven't worked a job since.

Haven't fully trusted myself.

I mean deep down, I wanted that guy to suffer. I couldn't help but imagine—what if those girls had been my sisters? Wouldn't I have wanted someone to step in? To protect them?

Maybe… just less brutally.

But either way, that man deserved what he got. Maybe even worse. Maybe he deserved to live in pain. Permanently.

That's why I didn't fully pull my punch.

That's why I was the monster.

Forever stuck as the made killer.

A sharp vibration in my hand pulled me back to the present. My phone buzzed; the screen dimly lit with Em's name. I blinked, pushing the past aside.

"Sean?"

I exhaled slowly, rolling my shoulders. "Uh-huh?"

"Did you hear me?"

I rubbed my temple. "Not at all."

"Fantastic!"

Em's sarcasm cut through the lingering fog in my head, grounding me back in reality.

I balanced the phone between my ear and shoulder, attempting to put on my shoes. "What did you say, Em?"

A pause. Then, a sharp breath. "Please don't 'Em' me."

I bit the inside of my cheek. "Shit! Fine! What did you say?"

"I asked what you wanted me to add and what company. Maybe I can include something specific to your résumé to make you stand out."

I exhaled, leaning back against the wall. "Just make it look like I haven't been off the face of the earth for the last few years."

"Uh-huh. And the company?"

"Hold up. I forgot what it was called. It's some development company or something."

There was a long pause.

"Of course, you applied to a place you know nothing about. Might want to know the name before your interview."

I could hear the smirk in her voice.

"No shit!"

"I'm just saying. It would be awkward if you messed up the company name."

I rolled my eyes. "Shut up. It's Crane Industries."

The name hung in the air for a second.

Ah yes - Crane Industries. The father-son empire that owned half the city. They sold properties, developed the rundown parts of the city, had several businesses, and imported products from Normalis – or what Grandpa Spencer used to call Europe.

But at least the rebranded "Normalis" made sense. Homo normalis. The so-called ordinary humans. Their way of distinguishing themselves from people like me—or from the supernaturals who had claimed America as their own.

At least we didn't try to rename the country. Minus the cities, of course.

Em's voice cut through my thoughts. "How did you get an interview with Crane Industries?"

I shrugged, even though she couldn't see me. "I don't know. I was just applying to random places, and they popped up. Who even knows if I'll get the job."

"Oh, YOU ARE getting that job. I am not wasting my time for you to not get the job."

"How nice of you," I scoffed.

"I'm just being a good sister."

I smirked, shaking my head. "Tch! Yeah a good adoptive sister."

"That's rude! We're a lot closer than that, and you know it!" Her voice wavered.

My jaw clenched. "We have the same half-sister and that's it. You're just as close as any of our other adoptive siblings, like Naomi and Bexley. That's it!"

"Why are you such an asshole?!"

Em's voice cracked a little.

I sighed, pinching the bridge of my nose. "I'm just being honest with you. Which is something Waverly told us to do with each other."

"Well, you could have fibbed a little and not said it so cruelly."

She sounded upset now. But I wasn't going to lie to her, I couldn't.

"It would have been more cruel of me to lie to you."

A pause.

Her tone flattened now. Guarded. "Okay, whatever. I'm done with your resume, was that all you needed?"

"Um – yeah, I believe so."

"Great, please don't call me again."

"Hey wait, thank you for-"

The line clicked. She hung up.

I shouldn't be surprised she hung up on me. I was cruel to her, so it was only fair she was cruel to me. Still, it just sucked a little that she didn't wait for me to thank her. Not that she would've expected it. She probably didn't even realize I was going to.

Either way, it was good she hung up on me. She didn't need to be caught up in the person I've become. Em had more going for her, a future that didn't involve bloodstained hands or sleepless nights haunted by the things we'd done. Her ability kept her from stepping into the field, but that didn't stop the higher-ups from putting her behind a screen—guiding us through missions, directing our movements, keeping us alive. And she was damn good at it.

And at least she never had to witness the true horrors of the field. Never had to watch the light fade from someone's eyes.

Sure, she still had blood on her hands, being the brain behind some of our assassinations made her an accomplice. But it wasn't the same as physical blood.

It wasn't the same as holding someone down while they gasped their last breath.

Another reason it was good she hung up.

I had just arrived at the skyscraper—the towering headquarters of Crane Industries.

I had been standing outside for five minutes, locked in conversation, barely acknowledging where I was. If she hadn't ended the call, I probably would have kept talking to her and missed my interview altogether.

I pulled at my shirt, hoping to smooth out some of the wrinkles, exhaled slowly, and glanced up at the massive glass structure. The reflection of the city stretched across its sleek surface, the building standing as a silent reminder of power and control.

Despite my cold nature and my usual emotionless tone, I actually enjoyed talking with my adoptive sister. Her attempts at being sassy and cold were almost comical. And her voice—normally soft, soothing, familiar—always had a way of warming my stomach.

Though today, she had been sharper with me. Colder.

I deserved it.

But still, it reminded me that I had moments in my childhood that weren't all bad.

Faint, distant memories of warmth.

Tiny specks of light in the darkness of my past.

And for that, I had my adoptive siblings to thank.

But I would never admit that aloud.

Vulnerability.

I shoved the thought aside as I took a step forward. But she didn't stay and I reluctantly walked into the skyscraper for my interview.

The moment I walked in, the faint hum of productivity filled the air—muted conversations, and the occasional shuffle of shoes against polished floors.

The front foyer was big, decorated in a way that screamed wealth and status with dark wood paneling, sleek modern furniture, and a reception desk that looked more like a high-tech command station.

Several workers moved through the space, dressed in crisp suits and calculated smiles, all seemingly eager to assist me. One of them, a security guard at the front desk, was generous enough to guide me to the interview hallway.

Glad to know I wasn't the only man unsure of where he was going in this colossal building.

As a quiet thank you, I tried to slip him a tip for his assistance.

He refused. A smile tugged at the edges of his face as he shook his head. "Don't bother."

Apparently, the gesture alone was enough. He appreciated the offer, especially since most men who walked through those doors hadn't even tried to do the same. Some didn't even bother to thank the security guard.

To make matters even more shocking, he chuckled and told me, "Your parents must have raised you right."

My stomach twisted. He had no fucking clue what my life was actually like. My gentlemanly nature was a façade.

Just another mask people wore. Only my mask was professionally made. Underneath the suit, the polite nods, the carefully calculated words, I was still the same.

I would always be a killer in disguise.

I mean, Waverly and Kayta tried their best to give us a proper and fortunate childhood. Ultimately they couldn't stop the program from running – corrupting our innocence. At least they were there to chase away the nightmares, taught us ways to cope and decompress as well as taught proper things that children should learn. Waverly and Kayta made us into family, despite the trauma that came with it.

But I would never be a true gentleman.

I pushed open the frosted glass door leading to the waiting area. I had expected professionalism. Instead, I was greeted with self-entitled brats lounging in expensive chairs, scrolling through their phones, adjusting their designer cufflinks, or gossiping in low murmurs about last night's exclusive party.

Nepo-babies.

Spoiled brats.

Most of them were only here because Mommy and Daddy threatened to cut off their credit cards. None of them had ever known real sacrifice.

They didn't understand the reality of the working class. The ones who fought for every dime. The ones who bled for their paychecks. The ones whose existence didn't come with an inherited safety net.

I knew assholes like these guys. I had worked for their parents. Parents like theirs were the ones who hired me and my family. It wasn't about necessity.

It was about power.

It was about proving a point.

Look what we can afford.

A child assassin.

Don't fuck with us.

We have money.

Completely and utterly pathetic, but if you've got the money, who's going to stop you from using it? I can't even remember the amount of times I was hired just so someone could flex their wealth—to prove that they had enough cash to buy death itself.

And then there were the ones who used us to eliminate their competition.

They hired us, prayed that their rivals weren't doing the same, and if they were?

They prayed harder that they had more money.

That was the real game.

Not skill. Not intelligence. Not talent.

Just money.

It was almost insane how many of the guys in this room would probably kill or hurt each other if given the chance. Hell, some of them probably already had. I could see it in their eyes—the way they measured each other up like pieces on a chessboard.

How many of them had used Mommy and Daddy's money to get rid of academic, athletic, or romantic competitors?

Way too many. But I guess when you've got the money and unlimited resources, anything is possible.

Don't get me wrong, I've got money too. Hard earned money, but money nonetheless. I admit, had I been raised as sheltered and spoiled as half these guys, I'd be spending it just as stupidly and selfishly. I never got a childhood like that — like I've been saying this whole time. Besides, it didn't help that I was always on the receiving end of dealing with rich people and their excess wealth. So no, I probably wouldn't end up like them.

Then again, I didn't allow myself to access my money that easily. Not because I couldn't. Because I wouldn't. Why? Because I refused to let myself spend it as recklessly as these people did. And I sure as fuck wouldn't waste it on hiring assassins just to get rid of a competitor.

I wouldn't have hired people like me.

Wouldn't have spent a dime to traumatize kids the way my adoptive siblings and I were traumatized.

A voice cut through my thoughts. "Sean Barnes?"

Well, at least I didn't have to wait that long with these rich dickwads. Or maybe I am late and these guys are going through another round of the interview process.

I straightened my jacket. "Yeah, I'm here."

The lady barely looked at me as she turned. "Follow me, sir."

I couldn't imagine what it would be like to be an assistant or secretary. On one hand, you were just cleaning up someone else's messes. On the other hand, you were practically babysitting a grown adult, getting their food, beverages, making appointments for them, and even dressing them for occasions. Secretaries were just overpaid babysitters who chose this job because they hoped to be successful one day, but instead, they settled for the bottom of the ladder. They convinced themselves that once they learned from the big boss, they'd climb higher. That their boss would put in a good word for them when the time was right.

It was entirely pathetic.

Though I won't say that's how all of them are, but at least 95% of them fit the mold. Trust me, I had dealt with enough secretaries to know.

So the question was, which one was this woman? The 95% who think they'll climb the professional ladder? Or was she part of the 5%, contented to be an adult babysitter?

The clicking of her heels on the polished floor matched the confident, steady tone of her voice. "What made you choose this lovely company?" I asked, glancing at her.

She didn't even hesitate. "Sir, I am not the one who you will be speaking with."

I smirked. "I figured, but if I'm going to work here, I would want to know the other staff."

She gave me a sidelong look, unimpressed. "Very cocky of you to assume that you'll be hired."

"On the contrary, I'm just being confident. Besides, I think I'll be a great choice."

"What makes you so sure?"

I tucked my hands into my pockets, glancing at the other applicants behind us, still waiting. "I'm not here to impress mommy or daddy. And I'm not trying to get their foots in the high society door just because I work for Crane Industries."

"Is that what you think? Do you think everyone here is trying to impress their parents?"

I arched a brow. "Wouldn't you say so? Most of these guys are probably here for experience before taking over their parents' companies."

"What about you then?" she challenged. "Not trying to impress or help out 'mommy or daddy', as you said?" she added.

"Don't got either to impress."

"Surely you do, I can see it."

I gave her a blank look. "How so?"

"You act like you have no one to impress like you're above the others."

Trust me, lady, I know I'm not above any of them. They didn't have half the problems I have. They didn't have the trauma I have.

"Everyone is trying to impress someone," she continued. "Or prove someone wrong. You are no different. Chances are, you are trying to do something that involves mommy and daddy too."

She wasn't entirely wrong. She had a point. Technically, I was doing this to stop wasting away in my apartment. And sure, Waverly expected me to get a job again. But I had no plans to admit that all to this stranger.

I shrugged. "Possibly or possibly not. Like I said got neither to impress."

She smirked. "Sure, sure."

I glanced at her. "Does that mean you are one as well?"

"Yes I am. I have no fear in admitting that. I'm here to impress my family. Especially my father."

I tilted my head slightly. "I wish you the best of luck with that."

"He has been invested in my time with the company and been impressed with the work I've been doing. So I think I'm doing good."

I didn't ask, nor did I really care.

She lifted her chin slightly, her voice carrying a quiet sense of pride. "I think I'll move up in the company soon."

She was definitely in the 95% range—the ones with hope to move up. Guess she didn't know her place.

How sad.

"Sounds like you have big plans." I remarked.

"Big plans indeed —" she answered.

Damn, could she just stop? She was just proving my point further.

"Oh gosh, I'm sorry for going on and on. This is the room where you'll be interviewed," she said, gesturing to the door.

"Thank you so much, miss."

The words left a bitter taste in my mouth. I could only fake politeness for so long. I was a cranky man a with little joy in my life. Plus, once she started talking, she was too perky.

If I were to get hired, I will avoid asking her questions. I wasn't sure I could maintain my kind facade that long — man, that woman could talk and talk for hours. Makes you feel almost sorry for her. I mean, it just showed how alone she really was, spilling her goals and dreams to a complete stranger.

It's sad.

I suppose I should feel bad for her. But I wouldn't know where to begin expressing that to her. I really don't want or need to come across as creepy if I did try to express my sympathy. That's the last thing I needed.

"Mr. Barnes?" a voice interrupted my thoughts.

I snapped back to paying attention, especially since I'm trying to get this job.

"Yes, that is me. Are you George Crane?" I asked, extending my hand.

"Unfortunately, that is my father," he replied, shaking my hand. "I am Damien Crane and will be conducting the interview, alongside my sister, Heather. But I'm sure you two have already met."

Makes sense now. She had thrown off my percentage though. I guess there is now a 1% that both tries to impress daddy and is comfortable in the position of babysitting her brother.

"Well, it's nice to meet you both." I said, forcing a smile.

"Before we start," Damien continued, "We would like to offer you this time to disclose anything. Our company believes in giving everyone a fair chance, so we open the floor for you to talk freely."

Weird, but okay.

"We also, do not expect you to have experience as a bodyguard, so please do not worry Mr. Barnes." Heather added.

"Please call me Sean, my grandfather goes by Mr. Barnes."

"Of course, Sean. Is there anything you need to disclose before we begin?"

My mind raced with thoughts I could possibly share:

That I'm a killer — no.

That I can't protect anyone — probably not a good idea to say that.

I have more blood on my hands than a serial killer — that would land me in a psych ward.

That I don't actually need this job — then why am I here?

Probably shouldn't say anything that would incriminate myself.

"I can't think of anything at the moment."

"Of course, we understand that sudden questions can catch people off guard," Heather replied, her tone surprisingly empathetic.

I guess she wasn't too bad.

"Sometimes," Damien added with a light chuckle, "People become nervous and blurt out every dark secret they have."

Why would he say that? His voice was light, but there was an unsettling seriousness beneath it. Did he enjoy making people uncomfortable? Was this some sort of power play? A dominance assertion?

Well, I can easily say, that I wasn't one to divulge my secrets. Plus, I'm not the type of person who keeps or shares secrets—people just don't do that with me.

"You sure there's nothing you want to tell us?" he pressed, his eyes glinting in a way that made my skin crawl.

Yeah totally — no thanks. That was way creepy, man.

"No secrets here, Mr. Crane."

"That's too bad. I guess we'll start the interview then."

Why would that be bad?

This was getting weird.

Something didn't seem right.

He didn't seem right.

There was something about the glisten in his eyes that put me off, making his smile ten times more creepy.

Trust me, I learned the ability to read body language, detect subtle ticks, and notice changes in tone — skills essential for survival in my line of work. You never know when you would need to protect yourself and kill – if that was needed.

Damien Crane had an unsettling aura; I could see it. Some ulterior motive, but I wasn't sure what it was. I wasn't a mind reader. Though I wished that was my ability instead—never having to get actual blood on my hands with that power. Oh, how much easier work would have been. Though I think that my adoptive sister Bex racked up the most kills and hires out of any of us — she was never going to need a job for her retirement. Also, I think she was probably the least traumatized out of all of us. I mean, there was no actual blood on her hands, maybe just stained in her brain.

Stained on her soul like the rest of us.

Reading this guy's probing expression, I anticipated his next question.

"Have you worked as a security detail before?"

"Yes, I used to work as a bouncer."

He nodded. Heather jotted down a note and asked. "What did that entail?"

I shifted slightly in my seat, recalling the countless nights at the club. "Monitoring the clients that came in and out of the club, making sure no fights broke out, and providing safety for those who wanted or needed it."

"Did you work independently or as a team?"

"Depends on the night."

He raised an eyebrow, prompting me to elaborate. "Explain?"

I continued, "On busy nights, like Thursday to Sunday, there would be more of us — more clients were around those days. But on Tuesdays and Wednesdays, only one of us would be on duty and that was mostly me."

Heather's slightly raised her brow. "You only got one day off?"

I nodded. "Working helped me."

He titled his head, curiosity evident in his eyes. "Helped you how?"

I took a moment before I responded, carefully choosing my words "It helped in regulating my emotions and thoughts. Working keeps me from my impulses and lets me maintain a professional mindset."

His gaze sharpened. "Do you struggle with your mental health?"

I flinched slightly, not expecting the directness of the question. "I don't see how that would apply here." I replied, my tone edged with defensiveness.

"Are you on any medications?"

I shook my head. "No."

"Should you be on something?"

I leaned back, crossing my arms defensively. *What was his problem?* I couldn't help but think.

Those words did not reflect what I said, "I think the medical system is screwed and doctors prescribe medication to people with no illnesses. Plus, I think they neglect people who have serious mental health illnesses. But no, I don't believe I need to be medicated."

Heather's gaze remained steady, marking down my response. "Do we need to be worried about you?"

I quickly answered her, with my voice firm. "No. I am stable, I can work."

I didn't actually believe they cared about the mental health of potential employees. They just wanted to make themselves look good by pretending to offer a helping hand, acting as if they would hire someone with a serious illness. But I honestly didn't think they would hire someone who was potentially unstable with their mental health.

He shifted gears and continued with his question. "Have you ever protected an individual as your sole duty?"

I furrowed my brow. "What do you mean?"

He clarified, "Let me rephrase. Have you ever only protected one person before?"

I shook my head. "No, I have protected groups of people."

He leaned in slightly. "How do you feel about fighting to protect someone?"

Without hesitation, I answered. "I can do it."

His next question was pointed. "Have you ever gotten in a fight as a bouncer?"

I nodded. "Yes."

He probed further. "Why?"

I maintained eye contact and explained. "A situation escalated and in the end, I defended the other customers and myself from a man." Why else would I get into a fight?

Damien's expression remained unreadable as he posed an unexpected question.

"Would you kill for someone?"

Wait...

Did I just hear that right?

I blinked, taken aback "I'm sorry?"

He repeated his words, "Would you kill for someone?"

I paused, considering my response, "It would depend on the person."

Then, Damien clarified, "It's to protect your boss from danger."

So, I elaborated, "I meant the person I would be killing."

He responded, "Obviously, whoever poses the biggest threat."

I felt a surge of unease. I didn't like him—for sure.

"I would subdue them before I resort to murder."

Damien spoke in a straightforward tone. "Well, it wouldn't be murder."

I couldn't hide my discomfort. "Taking a life is murder."

This man's demeanor remained calm, too calm. He couldn't be serious. I mean who rationalizes murder?

He spoke with confidence. "Not if it's self-"

But Heather did not let him finish his sentence. "Damien that's enough!"

"No, it's not! I want to know if he would kill to protect me!"

I met his stare firmly. "No. I would not. No one life is worth more than another."

A fleeting thought crossed my mind. *Well, except for mine*. I would gladly trade my life to bring back someone from my past. Damien's response was concerning. "That's good to know."

Why would he say it like that? Dude! I didn't owe him anything, so why act like I was in a great debt and have to take people's lives just because he said so? Just because he was a spoiled rich kid with his daddy's company didn't mean his life was worth more than, say, a homeless person's. Sure, the homeless guy might not have lived the most honest life—not that I believed Damien had either—but at least he knew better than to waste money. Damien Crane needed to get off his high horse and realize he wasn't as important as he thought. Why was there always some arrogant son trying to take over his father's business and make demands from everyone around him?

His next question was even more surprising. "Would you be willing to die for your boss?"

I couldn't hide my surprise. Goddamn, what kind of job was this?

I replied candidly. "I would die protecting my boss, but not willing to die for him if he's making me a scapegoat."

Let's be honest, who truly wants to die for their employer? Probably nobody.

Damien leaned back, considering my words. "Interesting. Now our final question — why do you think you are the best fit for this position?"

I composed myself, delivering the rehearsed response. "Beyond my experience as a bouncer, I think this job will give me the opportunity to expand my knowledge in protecting and working with high-profile corporate entities. Additionally, it will allow me to give back by ensuring the safety of this company's leaders."

Sounded like a bunch of bullshit spewing from my mouth, but hopefully, they bought it.

Damien nodded. "Alright. Thank you."

He continued, "My sister and I will need time to discuss, if you would please return to the waiting room, we'll be right out to discuss with you and the other gentlemen further."

"Actually, if you don't mind, I'm going to step out for a quick smoke."

Truth be told, I didn't smoke. I don't smoke.

Heather smiled politely. "Of course, we shall see you soon."

I left the room, the weight of the interview crushing down on me. The questions had taken unexpected turns, exposing more about the company's culture than I had imagined. As I approached the building's exit, I couldn't shake the impression that I was entering a world more dangerous than I had anticipated.

<center>~~~</center>

This was insane. That man was insane. Who in their right mind would want me to kill for them? To die for them? Or to be a shield for them? I know that's what bodyguards are supposed to do — protect their client — but only to a degree. There's a line. One that should not be crossed. However, some people—those with more money than common sense—wanted more than just protection. They sought obedience. Loyalty. A pawn. He shouldn't be asking questions like that, though. If you really wanted someone dead, there's government programs that can help you accomplish that — file a fucking assassination claim if you must. Don't put blood on someone's hands just to be protected like some kind of royal.

Fucking rich, arrogant bastard.

I exhaled sharply, squeezing my fists as tightness built up in my shoulders.

Damn it, I think I need a smoke now.

This was such a stupid idea! Why did I think applying to a company with this much influence was a good plan? I should have just stayed in the shadows, applied for another bouncer gig, and kept my expectations low. I shouldn't have been so goddamn optimistic about applying to Crane Industries. I'm a fool. And worst of all? It seems like I couldn't escape my roots. Even with what seemed like an easy, harmless — for the most part — bodyguard job, it wasn't as easy as I thought.

Who the hell asks a question like that in an interview? But of course, I bet all those spoiled princesses in the waiting area ran with that shit. They probably nodded, smiled, and blindly agreed. Of course, they would say yes to that question — anyone desperate enough for a job would say yes. But it's incredibly apparent that none of them had ever taken a life before. At least, not with their own hands. They didn't have to live with the permanent stain left on their hands – not like me. I was somewhat lucky that my hands weren't permanently stained by the lives I took, that would make things rather difficult to explain.

You know, sometimes I wish everything could have been better. That I didn't have these memories. That I didn't carry this curse. I wish I could have done more with my life and become someone. I should have! But no. I could not have. I was only a former child assassin, and they did not have normal lives. I wish I could have.

A sudden blast of wind blew past me, pulling me from my thoughts.

My surroundings returned to focus—the tall skyscraper, the low hum of traffic, and the faint conversation of people passing by.

I was still around. Still trapped in this stupid reality.

I sighed and rolled my shoulders, trying to relieve the tension.

"Help!"
The cry sliced through the air. I froze.
"Help please!"

The voice was closer now—frantic, raw. My spine went rigid, instincts kicking in before my mind could catch up.
"Please!"
"Someone please!"
"Please just help me!"

"PLEASE somebody!"

"Yo! You! Yeah, you! Come here!"

I don't know why I called this random, tattered girl over to me. Probably just trying to get her to shut up. She interrupted my self-deprecating thoughts—the very thing that kept me going during the day.

"What's your problem? What do you need?"

That came out way harsher than I meant. Her hands trembled as she grabbed my sleeve.

"You have to help me!"

"Yeah, I got that from all the "helps" you pleaded." My voice was dry, unimpressed. "What do you need help with?"

Sean, stop being a dick! Have you never heard of being cordial to strangers?

She inhaled sharply, looking over her shoulder, her entire body tense with paranoia.

"They're going to sell me!" Her voice dropped into a breathless whisper. "Or at least that's what they did with the others!"

"What?" My spine stiffened. "Who's going to sell you? Who are the others?"

Her eyes darted behind me, then back. "The warden and the men he works for, that's who want to sell me!"

"Who?"

I sounded like a fucking owl.

She let out a frustrated sigh. "Look sir! I don't have much time. I knocked out the warden and by now the rest will be looking for me. Can you help me or not?"

I narrowed my eyes. "I can, but I need more answers. Like who did this? I mean, look at you. You're bleeding badly. Your leg—your jeans are soaked."

Her jaw clenched. "The warden did that. He likes to hurt me."

"What?" My stomach twisted.

"What kind of person does that? Why?"

She took a shaky step closer. "Sir! I'll answer your questions after you get me away from here. Please!"

I exhaled sharply, running a hand through my hair. "Okay, let me hail you a cab."

She scoffed, shaking her head. "A cab? You're joking, right?"

"What's wrong with a cab?" Her deadpan demeanor almost had me laughing.

"They won't let me in dressed like this. Plus, I'm bleeding, remember."

I looked at her again. I honestly didn't see anything wrong with her clothes. Sure, they were dirty, with blood on her pants, and severely ripped, but at least all the inappropriate parts were covered. But even though I genuinely saw no problem, I still offered my coat to her. I don't know why I did that. Yet, she took it without hesitation and quickly wrapped it around her tattered shirt.

"Do you want a cab?"

She hesitated, shifting her weight like she was considering running again.

"Can't you just take me in your car?"

I looked at her and said, "I don't have a car. I walked here."

Her brows lifted. "You walked here? What kind of person does that?"

I smirked. "Hmmm…Someone who lives around the corner."

She frowned and crossed her arms, but her hands continued to tremble. So, I asked. "Do you want the cab or not?"

She let out a heavy breath. "I guess if that's all you can give me."

I narrowed my eyes. "You know you don't have to take it."

Why was she being so picky? Like, take the damn cab or don't.

Why did I care so much?

She swallowed hard, glancing over her shoulder again, and this time, her voice cracked. "Please! I'll take the cab."

Finally. I nodded. "Okay just hold that-"

"Grab her!"

"Get her now!"

Her eyes dilated, and her entire body froze.

"They've come for me!" She grabbed my sleeve, her grip like a vice.

"Please don't let them take me!"

Damn, I couldn't deal with tears. Why did she have to cry?

I inhaled sharply, already regretting my actions. "Just stand behind me. Let me take care of this."

Her grip tightened. "They'll try and kill you."

I almost laughed. "Not out here, they won't."

A group of three or four men, dressed in spotless suits, pushed through the scattered crowd. They moved purposefully and precisely. You can tell they have been trained. The man in front was tall, with salt and pepper hair and steel eyes. He definitely nailed the "if looks could kill". He stepped forward and spoke in a tone that hardly masked his authority.

"Sir, please step away. This woman is highly dangerous."

I snorted. "I doubt that!"

I could sneeze, and she would probably fall over. She was too malnourished, her frame too weak and her hands trembling too much to be a real threat. Whatever they had done to her, they had made sure she was too weak to fight back. It made sense if they were planning to sell her. Deprive her of what she needed, and she'd lose the physical and mental fight in her.

"I am sorry sir, but you need to step back." His voice had a sharper edge now. The kind of voice that is used before a fight. This just got interesting.

His hand moved to reach for his weapon. Was he really going to try something? Here? With all these witnesses?

"Look, you need to listen. I'm not moving."

My voice was calm. Too calm.

I noticed how his jaw clenched and an expression of frustration in his eyes.

"Sean Barnes! What are you doing?" The voice sounded familiar.

"Oh no."

I think that was the first time I heard genuine fear in this girl's voice. Even when she was calling for help, she didn't sound this frightened. So why now? Was it because of him? Was it because of Damien Crane? What was wrong with this guy?

"Hey Sean, buddy, why don't you just step away from the girl and leave these men to deal with her." That voice. Smooth. Friendly. Too easygoing. Like we were just two guys discussing weekend plans instead of the life of a terrified girl.

"Sean, don't let them take me. Please?" She sounded fragile.

The fuck. What was this feeling? Why did I feel like I needed to help her? I wasn't a hero. I had never saved anyone.

I was a killer for fuck's sake. So why did I care so damn much?

"Sean! Step away!"

I tilted my head. "What happens when I move, hm?"

"They put me back in a dark room and will try to sell me later." She whispered.

I really hope none of these other men could hear her.

"They'll take her somewhere where she can't hurt herself or others." His voice was patient and condescending. As if he were explaining something simple to a child.

"If you haven't noticed, she's a bit unstable and delusional. She says crazy things like she's been abducted and going to be trafficked. Or that she's been locked in a dark room, but let's be honest, she's been getting her vitamin D. So trust me, she is very delusional." He acted like this was some big misunderstanding.

"I'm not. I swear I'm not." Her voice cracked, barely holding on.

Any normal person would see he had a point — to an extent of course. She could have been all those things he said, and yes, her story does have some parts that don't make any sense. But one thing I'm certain, she's definitely never been locked in a dark room. I knew what that looked and felt like. I know how disorientated you can be coming outside after that long in the dark. She was not even fazed. But the gnawing feeling I felt from Damien was enough to make me believe her. Something about him seemed strange. The instant I laid eyes on him, an uneasy feeling landed in my gut, indicating that something was seriously wrong with that guy.

"Please-"

"You don't want to cause a scene, do you?"

That's the thing, neither of us could make a scene. Crane Industries would suffer from a scandal if they attacked me, and I would risk exposing myself and who I was if I fought back. And I didn't need more blood on my hands.

"C'mon pretty boy, we don't got all day." The stone-cold man spat.

Pretty boy? Should I be insulted by that?

"Please don't-"

"I'm sorry, but I have to." The words tasted bitter on my tongue.

As I stepped away, I felt a slight tug on my shirt. Her grip was weak, shaky, desperate. But I didn't turn back. I couldn't.

Not with how guilty I felt.

I really wish I could have gotten her away from here sooner, but now her fate was in their hands.

I wish I could have done more. But I take lives, I don't save them.

"Good choice, avoiding unnecessary conflict. Just like you said in the interview."

The man from before stepped closer, his face unreadable as he walked to her.

"Now move further away from Nova. Nova give back his jacket."

Nova. That's a rather interesting name. It didn't seem to fit her though.

"She can keep it," I muttered. "It'll keep her warm and covered up properly."

He rolled his eyes. "Fine! Nova, come with us."

Before she got too far from me, I grabbed her arm—gently. With my strength and her skinny arm, I would have broken it if I grabbed it any harder. She was definitely malnourished.

"I'm sorry for not doing better," I said under my breath, "but I hope my jacket will do a better job of protecting you."

Her lips parted, but before she could say a word, they pulled her away from me. No hesitation. Probably bruising her in the process. Also forcing her to match their fast pace, despite her barely being able to walk with her bleeding leg, just showed me how little they cared about her wellbeing. I should go after them. I should protect her.

"Sean, you made a smart decision stepping back."

"What will you do with her?"

A twisted smirk crossed his face. "That's classified, but just know she will be taken care of."

My hands curled into fists. "What the fuck does that mean!"

"None of your business."

He let out a low chuckle. "Now, I'm sorry to say you didn't get the job. Have a good day."

Fucking prick! Why would he say it like that? Screw him and that stupid company. I didn't even want to work for him. He's obviously fucked in the head.

"You too. Good luck with the company."

Fuck you, was what I really wanted to say. Plus, I hoped his new bodyguard couldn't protect him from shit.

Damien glanced back as he walked away, issuing a final warning. "Also I do ask you to proceed with discretion about what you saw here. The media doesn't need to target us anymore."

Right! Because a girl claiming she was kidnapped shouldn't be reported to the authorities. Maybe it's time I look into this.

I forced a smirk. "Of course. My lips are sealed."

As he disappeared through the glass door, the fake smile contorted into a grimace.

Would it be surprising if I end up coming back for her? Especially if I find out that all Nova said was true. My lips might remain shut, but my mind would never shut off. And I will uncover the truth. Not for a job. Nor a favor, but for reckoning.

Look out Crane Industries.

You know those moments that replay in our minds for as long as you live? The ones that crawl into bed with you and keep you wide awake, even when you are dead tired? I used to think my past kills were the only ghosts haunting my nights. But now… now I'm not so sure. I'd be lying if I said I didn't still have nightmares from the past. They still come uninvited. But lately, it's not the faces of the dead that wake me up. It's her—Nova. I see her over and over again. Dead because of me. Bleeding out, eyes wide, and silent. I couldn't take it!

I couldn't stop the guilt! It's rotting me from the inside. It was making me fucking sick! I couldn't even sleep knowing how I barely helped the girl. Not when I know I could've done more.

I should probably recheck the jacket, and make sure it hadn't moved or been thrown away. Thank God for Waverly's protectiveness. She never had to use it, but she put these circuits in the fabrics of our clothes that allowed us to be tracked, to monitor our health, and a bunch of other stuff — specifically to ensure we were still alive during missions. Now that most of us are out of the field, she doesn't check them as often, depending on the occasion. However, these articles of clothing make up most, if not all, of what we own. They were custom-made to fit our exact builds, even designed to grow with us. So, we never really had to buy anything else.

The jacket I gave to Nova? It wasn't just to keep her warm. I made sure to request access to track the circuit embedded inside. I'd also stuffed the pockets with snacks and a knife—essentials, really. You can never go wrong with that kind of stuff. God, I hope she found them. I hope she used them.

I should have done more for her.

I should be doing more for her.

Get up, you lazy shit. You have work to do.

I needed to check her location.

I wish I could check on her in person, but if what she has said is true, they have her held captive somewhere in the company's skyrise. There's no way they would let me see her.

But why? Why have her in captivity? Why isolate her from the outside world? Why hurt her?

What am I missing here?

They didn't even help bandage her leg. It's probably infected by now.

Why didn't I do more?

I pressed my finger on the call button again, as if pushing it hard enough would break the silence and bring her back.

"Em, pick up the goddamn phone!"

Ringing, again.

"C'mon!"

Click.

"What do you want now, Sean? I have a life too, you know."

I didn't waste time.

"I need your help looking into where Crane Industries gets most of its finances."

"Are you insane? Did you not just get hired there?"

"No, they rejected me for defending a girl they kidnapped."

There was silence, before she whispered, "What?"

I stood up, pacing the room. "Now, I want to know why they have her under lock and key!"

Her tone changed—sharpened. "You're serious? How do you know?"

"She has my jacket and hasn't left this one building in the last 35 hours."

There was a pause on the line. A silence that said she finally understood I wasn't just being dramatic.

"Okay, so you're very serious." Her voice dropped. "God, I feel so bad now. I'm sorry, Sean. But even if I could get into their system, I wouldn't fully know what I was looking for. Waverly always handled the payments from clients, not me. Plus, that system is too advanced for my hacking skills — they'd catch me the second I breached it."

"Em, please… you're so good. You're better than good"

"But I'm not the best Sean."

"I need someone really good. You don't get it, Em."

"What's going on, Sean?"

I clenched my jaw, forcing the words through the knot in my throat.

"I told her that I would help her" My voice cracked. "I said I would, and yet I stepped away before a fight broke out. I let them take her. I watched her get dragged off like she was nothing, I needed to help her. I promised her!"

"Sean—"

"Please! I can't eat without being sick. I can't sleep. I'm a fucking mess!"

There was another long pause. I hated this feeling. Letting her hear it. But I couldn't stop. I wouldn't stop. "Oh, Sean," she said softly. "Okay, I'll see what I can do. But I'm telling you, it won't be much."

"What about Naomi or Curtis?"

"You didn't hear?"

I paused. "Hear what?"

"Naomi's high school boyfriend passed away recently."

I blinked. "You mean the guy she was currently with?"

"Well yeah, but not anymore. Technically."

For someone who spent most of her time glued to a screen, Memory had a disturbing lack of emotional filter. Maybe it was her way of staying sane, but still, she was worse than most of us who had taken lives. It was almost like she had no feelings toward death, like it was something in her life constantly. Death didn't seem to shake her. She may have had the same trauma as us when it came to the facilities, but she never had to take a life. She wasn't made to take a life.

So then, why was she so callous when it came to family member's deaths?

Naomi's boyfriend was one of us. Sure, he wasn't born in a facility, not made into an assassin, but he too, struggled with his abilities. He was one of us!

"When did it happen?"

"A few months ago. Naomi has been out of commission since. Completely off the radar."

"No kidding. So, I guess Curtis is with her?"

"I'm not sure. He went off the grid weeks ago. His last location was off the coast of Francia, but I don't know why he was there."

I sighed. "Fantastic!"

"I'm so sorry, I really wish I could help-"

"Don't worry about it." I cut in. "I have an idea now."

"You aren't going to do anything stupid… right?"

"Probably not," I smirked, even though she couldn't see it. "I'll let you know, though."

"Sean-"

"Catch you later!"

I ended the call before she could try to talk me down. I was going to regret this plan. But honestly? I already knew that, but what choice did I have? My two adoptive siblings, who were the best of the best at hacking into systems, were awol and Memory wasn't good enough to do it. That only left one person with the expertise to pull off this stunt, and I had a feeling about how this would play out. I didn't have much of a choice, though! Especially if I desperately wanted to get to the bottom of this. Plus, this would probably help Nova out way better than I originally did.

I ran a hand down my face. Shit! I'm going to regret-

My phone buzzed in my hand. A familiar name lit up the screen.

Fuck! Why is she calling me? I exhaled and answered.

"Hi, darling!" Her voice was way too cheerful.

"Hey, mom."

"Do you want to tell me what's going on?" I froze.

How does she always know?

"What do you mean?"

"Well, you've been trying to call me for the past minute, plus, you keep backing out of actually dialing my number."

I blinked. "Are you watching me?"

"Of course not," she replied smoothly, "but I can see when people type my number in. And you've done it at least five times before I finally called you."

I sighed, the guilt already settling in. "I'm sorry. I was just debating if I should call you for help."

A pause. "And here I thought you wanted to talk with me — like to tell me you are alive."

"No, that's not why I called you."

Why did my voice become so soft? Almost sorrowful, as if I was being scorned. I mean, yes, she is technically my mother — an adopted mother who took me and others in when nobody else wanted us — and I should call regularly, but that's not who I am. I knew that! She knew that.

Then, why did it still hurt to let her down? I feel like a disappointment for not reaching out more frequently. I wasn't built for guilt, but somehow she was the only one who could make me feel it.

"I know," she said gently, "but you know it's a mother's wishful thinking. Now, how can I assist you, darling?"

I paused, studying the way she always slipped into that mothering tone.

It was never forced. Never fake.

How the hell did she do that with kids who weren't even hers by blood?

How did she always manage to sound... safe?

I forgot sometimes—how lucky I was to be found by her.

To be accepted. Raised.

To be loved when I didn't think I was worth the effort.

Maybe I should've shown more appreciation.

Actually, not even a maybe. I should have, without question.

"Sean, darling?"

"I'm sorry," I whispered, the words sticking to my throat. "I really am."

"What's going on?"

"I didn't want to drag you into this. I didn't want to drag any of you into this, but I need help. I don't know what to do!"

There was no judgment in her voice. Just warmth.

"Okay, darling, take a breath."

Inhale Sean. Just breathe. Now exhale. Inhale. Exhale.

"Is that better?"

"A bit."

"Good, now explain it to me, and take as many breaks as you need. I have all the time in the world to hear about this problem."

I wish I had a filter—I desperately wish I did. If I had, I would have stopped myself from telling her everything that happened, including all my morbid and questionable thoughts. I wish I had stopped talking. She knew too much. She couldn't know all of this. I couldn't have her know this side of me.

She couldn't know me.

Just shut up, Sean!

Stop talking!

Shut your fucking mouth!

STOP!

There was a pause. Her voice was calm, steady—like she hadn't just heard the worst parts of me. "Oh darling, you've been through too much stress these past few days."

Her tenderness made it worse. It cracked something open. "Mom?" A whisper. A confession. "Why do I feel so guilty?"

"Sean, you are human. No matter what anyone says, that is in your genes. And being human means you feel as though you should have done better, and trusted your instincts to help this girl. You let yourself feel her disappointment, and now you're wearing it like it's your own. That is why you feel so much regret and guilt."

"I'm a fail-"

"No." Her voice cut through mine like a warm blade.

"But just because you feel that way does not make it true. You might not have helped her at that specific moment, but look at you now. You're so worried over her, feeling desperate to help. I've never been more proud of you! You are willing to help her and people like her in this situation — stop doubting yourself and your ability."

"But how can I help Mom? I didn't get the job and probably am on a 'don't let in' list."

"Well, don't break into the place."

"…Then what should I do?"

"First, we look into who's financing them—who's keeping Crane Industries afloat. Then, we check for missing people reports across the country. If there's a pattern, we'll find it."

"We're going to figure this out. We're going to help those people. And we'll help her."

"You're going to help me?"

"Of course I am, darling!"

"Thank you, mom."

"Darling, I will always help you." Her voice softened. "You are my son. All you ever have to do is call and ask for help." That hit hard. Harder than I wanted to admit.

"Now," she said, slipping into her professional tone, "I will get you those reports by the end of the day. In the meantime, get some rest, darling. You know how impulsive you get when you're tired. Plus, you can't help Nova if you aren't one hundred percent."

"Thank you, mom."

"Rest well, darling."

I didn't understand how she did it. She had her biological children, yet she treated us as her own. Never once did she prioritize her actual children over us or vice versa. How does she do it? Why does she do it? All of us — the adopted children — are dangerous. Most of us are killers, yet she still loves us. We're still loved. She treats us no differently, even though we have blood on our hands! She loves us, yet I don't get why. Truly, why did she take us as her own? Why does she care so much about us?

Why care about me?

She shouldn't!

She really, shouldn't!

⁓ ⁓

Self-deprecation is easy when you've been built to destroy.

That's always been one way to help me sleep — especially with having a dreamless sleep. I'm not entirely sure why they were dreamless, but with all the built-up anger, resentment, and stress for myself being released, I was easily knocked out. It was probably a lot better than drinking myself to death or taking drugs to get the tiniest amount of rest. Yet, I already knew that Waverly would disapprove of my method.

Speaking of her. Did she send me anything? I checked my screen. I saw nothing.

I didn't see anything.

How long would it take, anyway? Or did something else come up?

She was a busy woman. She runs two companies. Something probably came up, and she had to attend to it. I shouldn't expect her to drop everything and assist with my problems or needs. She's a very busy woman.

I know better. I know how busy she gets.

I shouldn't have asked in the first place.

She is a busy woman, Sean!

Maybe I should check on Nova instead? See if they've moved her. That, at least, I could control.

Nope!

Of course, they haven't moved her!

Why would they? She was no threat to them…. Or maybe she was?

That pocket knife I slipped into the jacket would give her some sort of advantage against them.

Hopefully!

But she still has the jacket. Beyond that? I don't know anything.

I don't even know if she was really kidnapped or being sold off. I am just following what my gut was saying, and my gut tells me something's off. There was something twisted and dangerous about Damien Crane. I, for one, would always trust my gut on those types of people. And I know damn well Damien Crane was one of them. But Nova? My instincts didn't tell me anything about her. I didn't know whether I could trust her or not.

Why would anyone sell her? What was so special about her? Sure, she was pretty and probably had a unique personality, but why her? Why do people like her? Why kidnap and sell people? What does anyone get from that?

Obviously, money, Sean!

So, maybe I trusted her. At least a bit. But everything still seems a bit far-fetched. Why was she kidnapped and not sold right away? From what I've gathered from her story, multiple others were taken and sold, yet she remained. Why? Does no one want her? Has she done something that turns people from buying her? Or was this just bullshit, and she's crying for attention?

Why hadn't I heard about missing people in the area? Why haven't I seen posters for anyone missing? Why haven't I seen Nova's missing person poster?

Was it because it was fake?

Everything was a test? A test to make me look like a fool?

A test to see who I would choose to protect?

Well, Damien Crane, I chose the underdog over the rich asshole. I'd do it all over again, too!

That's why they didn't hire me. Not because I saw too much and heard something I shouldn't have, but because I failed their test. It was all one big test!

I wish I could genuinely believe that. It would make life so much simpler. But I couldn't believe it, I won't believe it. My instincts wouldn't have been screaming that much had it just been a test. So it couldn't be true! Plus, if it were some fucking test, why wouldn't they have said so afterward? Instead, Damien Crane told me not to talk about what I saw and not talk to the media specifically.

It makes you wonder why he would say that if it meant nothing. If she was lying? But why the media or reporters specifically? Did they have other allegations like this?

I get why they wouldn't want these rumors about their company. Yet if you really think about it, the story is far-fetched—no reporter or media outlet would report on this without proof. Plus, the companies would be too scared to report on this topic because they wouldn't want to be sued.

Damien Crane didn't want these media outlets involved. What if there had been reports on the company for this situation before? If that's the case, it would make sense that he didn't want this to get out—he wouldn't want to add more fuel to the fire.

No company wants to get exposed for human trafficking! Maybe I'm not that much of a fool for believing Nova after all.

There are too many sirens going off in my head—too many gut warnings—and every time I think about Crane Industries, about him, those alarms scream louder.

I don't believe a single thing that comes out of Damien Crane's mouth anymore.

Hell, now I think he was spinning bullshit the moment he opened it.

There's no way Nova was lying to me.

No way.

Now I've officially confused myself.

Deep down, I wanted to believe Nova. But there were still pieces that didn't fit. Things she said that didn't line up.

Then again... maybe that was just the disorientation—trauma messing with her memory. I would also admit that my distrust and dislike for Damien Crane and his company was fueling my trust in Nova's story.

Ever since he asked that stupid question — *would you kill for someone* — I hadn't felt the same. That was the moment something inside me snapped. Since then, my body has been a live wire, ready for a fight. Because a normal person or company would not ask such a question during an interview. It didn't matter what the job was, no one would ask it. Not the army, the secret service, the FBI, the CIA, or any fucking government job that would require life or death loyalty. Those jobs came with expectations, yes—danger, yes. But they would never asked it! People signing up for THOSE jobs knew the risks and requirements to keep people safe. They already knew what they were getting into. This pathetic bodyguard job should not require that type of action to protect the spoiled, little boss. And yet Damien Crane had the audacity to ask if I'd be willing to kill for him.

It was insane to ask such a thing to potential employees.

He was fucking insane!

No wonder I believed the young girl, who claimed she was kidnapped by his bullshit empire!

Yup, I've officially lost my mind!
Maybe, I needed a hobby or something.
Something that wasn't destructive and wouldn't kill me in ten years—assuming I even made it that long.
So what should I do?

Join a sports team?
Who was I kidding? I'd probably end up killing everyone in the field.
What about painting? Drawing?
Never mind, I hated the tedious nature of both.
Carpentry?
Could be fun, as long as I don't end up with a nail or screw in the hand again. That was the first and last time I ever worked a job at a construction site. The victim was also one of the first people who ever fought back, then I finished the job by tossing him off the fifteenth floor.
What about something simple? Like hobbies, something I can do with just my hands?
Waverly always thought I should do crochet or knitting. But let's be honest, there was no chance that I would sit down and knit to calm myself. I would rather put a gun in my mouth than be sitting around with string and two fucking sticks.
So no. Not many hobbies out there that I wanted to do.
I could always go back to working out to help with my destructive emotions, but I've been working out since I could walk. So that was out of the question.
I couldn't keep doing it.
I couldn't be stronger!

The more I work out, the stronger and deadlier I get.

Couldn't have that!

I wouldn't have that!

What should I do?

What COULD I do?

I hated waiting around, especially when I didn't know how long I'd be waiting.

Fuck!

Maybe I should go for a walk. Or better—go for a jog. Something light. Just enough to burn time. And hey, if I just so happened to pass by the Crane Industries skyrise while I was out… well, that'd be a coincidence. Right?

But I just said I shouldn't work out.

But then again…jogging was barely a workout if you think about it. What would be the harm? Plus it would allow me to pass the building without looking like I had a vendetta and too much free time. Jogging it was then! Even if I did despise it.

It was one of the few exercises I wasn't forced to do often, and yet I forced myself to do it religiously, much like the other exercises. I realized that even though the facility and my coordinators didn't force me to do cardio, I would eventually have to do it, especially if I was running after targets. So what became my least frequent workout, ended up being something I did all the time. My cardio went from nothing to running 50 km a day. After that, no targets ever had the opportunity to outrun me ever again — not that it ever happened. Better to be safe than to lose money after not being able to catch the target.

It happened to one of the assassins at Waverly's compound, and he could never live it down—he was always known as the assassin who couldn't catch his target.

I think he took his life after his failed mission.

Looking back, I felt bad for the guy. Getting picked on by a bunch of children wasn't anyone's idea of fun—especially not for a middle-aged man. But he wasn't like us — he wasn't trained from birth to be a killing machine, nor did he have abilities. It's no wonder he felt inferior. Assassins, being half or even three-quarters younger than you, would do anything to a man's ego, especially if they did your job ten times better and got chosen to complete more assignments than you.

I felt guilty knowing that he felt the only option for him was to take his life. But the life of an assassin always felt like we had no other purpose when we weren't given jobs. That and the trauma it gave you. It's rather surprising that none of us — my adoptive siblings and I — had done the same as he had done. Then again, my siblings found other purposes in their lives, ones that let them keep on living.

I haven't.

So then, why am I still alive?

Why haven't I given up?

I should have by now, right?

Yet here I was stalking, I mean jogging, past Crane Industries to see if they were up to no good, just for a girl I barely met.

Surely, that makes total sense, Sean!

You're an idiot!

No normal person would do this sort of thing!

Quite a stupid man, Sean!

Would it be too late to go back?

Just to jog back home and stay there until I wasted away.

Why did I have to help this girl?

Why did I feel the need to protect her?

Why am I so stupidly insane?
Quite a stupid boy, huh Sean?
Stupid. Stupid. Stupid!

But now I'm here. At this stupid building. And since I was already there, I might as well have continued my jog around the area — more specifically, around the building. Obviously, nobody would be kidnapped or sold at the front of the building, so I made my way to the back of the building I. Either way, they were kind of doing a poor job of hiding the fact they were taking people. Yes, Nova's claims may sound far-fetched, but they weren't doing anything to deny her claims.

Yet, as soon as I turned around towards the back of the building, all my doubts about Nova diminished. As I rounded that corner, I was greeted with the sounds of cries, begs, and grunts. Which only grew louder the closer I got to the back. I wasn't sure if they were from pain or annoyance, but from the sound alone, I couldn't tell how many people there were. I knew there had to be quite a few judging by how loud the sounds were getting as I got closer. Yet, I still wanted to get a visual. But getting close enough to see without being seen? That was going to take some effort.

That's the one thing I was never good at —no matter how hard I trained for it. I was never one to be a stealthy guy. So at this moment, I need to be careful. I couldn't risk being caught. They wouldn't let me walk away a second time. And let's be honest—if they did catch me? They'd either sell me off or kill me on the spot just to keep their secret operation out of the spotlight.

I had to be quiet, as quiet as I could manage, and try to get that visual. Better yet, a photo. Something I could actually use as proof. But I wouldn't be that lucky. I was never that lucky. Plus, even if I had put the image on the Internet, people would call me a liar and believe it to be some computer-generated image. I needed hard evidence like bank statements and physical accounts of people being taken. That sort of thing is to show people the truth. Even then, people still might not believe it.

People always found it difficult to believe the hard truth.

It was stupid. So stupid!

Come on, people, open your fucking eyes! Look at the world around you!

Look at what was fucking happening!

Okay, Sean, stop focusing on the future! You need to examine everything thoroughly before making assumptions.

Get a visual!

Well, I would've loved to have, except some man and his little kid came running around the building straight at me. I quickly put my finger up to my mouth so that they didn't freak out that I was there.

"Dipshit! Watch all of them, or else they'll run!"

"Don't forget to count them! Dipshit, we need them all to be here."

Another voice chimed in casually, like they weren't talking about actual human lives.

"Yeah, we don't get paid if that's the case"

Before I could process it, the man in front of me spoke—this time, more desperate.

"Excuse me, can you help us? Help my boy?"

Why does everyone want my help? Why did I put myself into these situations?

"Please, can you—"

I felt bad for cutting him off, but the man, who I couldn't see, piqued my interest. His obnoxious voice was one I could never forget after this. It was like nails on a chalkboard; it would always make me cringe thinking back to it.

"Are you kidding me?!"

Oh, this was about to get interesting.

"What do you mean you counted twelve people? We were supposed to have fourteen! Are you kidding me?!"

The man beside me tugged at my arm.

"Please, sir?"

I lowered my voice. "Just stay behind me. I'll help you, but you have to wait. I have to see what's happening first."

"They'll be looking for us soon," the boy whispered.

"How many men are there watching and escorting you?"

"There's three. Two handlers and one supervisor."

A voice snapped from around the corner. Loud and agitated.

"Dipshit and Dingus! Stay here while I go find those two. They couldn't have gotten far."

The man beside me grabbed my arm again, panic rising in his voice.

"Please, you have to help. He's coming. Please?"

"Just stop talking and be quiet." I snapped, barely above a whisper.

Then I glanced down at the kid—wide-eyed, clinging to his father. "Oh, and make sure your son doesn't see this."

I didn't hear exactly what the man said, but I'm pretty sure it was something like 'What are you about to do?' but I didn't bother explaining and jogged over the corner right as the loud man rounded it.

He looked surprised to find someone standing on this side of the wall. I couldn't blame him, had I too been looking for a father and son, I would have never expected to find someone like me around the corner. But that was just my assumption to what he was thinking.

I never let him get over his initial surprise before I grabbed him.

Maybe I should have given him a chance to run? But did he ever let any of those people run? No! So, maybe my choice wasn't the worst idea.

I think I should have held back. The grip I had on his shoulder was enough leverage to push him into the wall beside us. Based on his stature, I figured he would have at least remained conscious after he made impact – my assumption was wrong. He crumpled down against the wall instantly.

Maybe not the brightest decision on my side. I could have killed him. I might have killed him. Maybe I should make sure he was still breathing. But from what I could see, the wall had no dent nor blood, I'm sure he was just knocked out.

I did my best in sounding like the ringleader. "Oi! Dipshit and Dingus!"

I was glad I had the element of surprise. I know for damn sure I would've been able to fight them head-on, but I didn't want to. They had guns and probably knives, but I didn't see those. Getting the element of surprise allowed me to get to them before they had time to draw their guns or even react. I was next to them before they even registered, I wasn't the loud man. In seconds, I had their heads knocked together.

One fell like a sack of rocks — he took the brute impact. Meanwhile, the other stumbled away, only to be tackled by me and receive a couple of punches before he was knocked out.

Why was my first instinct always to fight?

Let's be honest, the last time I tried to talk to these guys, Nova got taken. So my new motto was to fight and talk later, if they're still awake.

"Only the three, right?"

Silence

"Are you all deaf? Are there more guys or not?"

A shaky voice finally replied. "Oh, umm, no, sir."

"No, what!"

"No, there aren't any more men."

"Ok, great then. Why are you still here? Why aren't any of you running?"

I looked at them, eyes wide, frozen like deer in headlights. "I'm here to get you out of here, so run!"

Of course, no one moved. They probably thought this was some cruel joke from their captors and didn't want to risk running. I can understand where they were coming from, but I doubt any of them would knock out their buddies.

So me yelling at them, obviously wasn't working.

"I'm looking for Nova. Is she here?"

A woman stepped forward, cautious but curious. "How do you know Nova?"

"No guards ever learned our names."

"Lucky for you. I'm not a guard. I met Nova the other day, and because I couldn't help her then, I thought I could come to help her now."

Obviously didn't happen.

"She's not here. They haven't found a buyer for her."

Fantastic!

Fucking great!

What really baffled me, though, was the fact that the man from earlier was still here. I mean, I figured he and his son would've bolted the second I knocked out the first guy. Call me, Elio Reed — you know that one athlete famous for running Nürburging in just under five minutes — that's how quick I would've been gone if I were him.

"Fuck!"

His voice pulled me back. "Why did you help us? I mean, it's rather obvious Nova isn't here."

"I didn't know she wasn't here at first, either way, I came to help."

"Come on, people, let's get you out of here, away from this hell hole. I figured you'd be jumping for joy to get out of here."

Someone from the back spoke up— hesitantly. "Can we trust you?"

"You shouldn't trust anyone, but right now, I'm the best shot you have getting out of here and not getting sold." I looked them dead in the eyes.

"But we shouldn't trust you?" one of them asked, hesitant.

"Sounds rather redundant, but I'm just trying to help."

"What do you get out of helping us?"

"Do you know how about I answer that when we're much further away from this place, m'kay?"

Smart of them not to object — wouldn't do that much if they did.

"Great, follow me!"

"Do we have to?"

"'Course not. You're free to do whatever you want."

Most, if not, all of them took off after I said that, not that I would blame them. At least a few did hang back and joined me when I suggested to move locations to a coffee shop several blocks over.

I figured those guys who work for the company wouldn't head to a specific coffee shop as they searched for this group. They probably head to the airport to intercept them — of course, that would be if they weren't found at their places of residence. Trust me, I knew how desperate these people were to get back on the right track. Their skins were on the line.

I knew how places like these worked.

I also figured that these people were probably hungry and needed caffeine, even if it was only three people. Plus, I was hungry. After all the effort I did taking those men out, whatever food I had in my system was long gone, and there wasn't a lot of it to begin with.

I sighed, and I stared at these three people, who were now staring back at me like I had all the answers. "Where do I begin with you guys?"

"You could answer Arthur's questions first."

I raised an eyebrow. "Oh yeah, what would those questions be?"

Arthur spoke, his voice steady but suspicious. "What are you getting out of helping us?"

I exhaled slowly, considering how much truth they could handle. "Ok, I'll be honest. I just want answers. I need to understand."

A younger girl squinted at me, arms folded tightly across her chest. "You're not trying to be a hero?"

I laughed under my breath and sounded bitter. "Sweetie, I'm far from being a hero."

She immediately bristled. "Don't call me, sweetie!"

I held up a hand in mock surrender. "Fair enough, noted," but I didn't apologize. Why should I? It was an honest mistake, and I shouldn't have to explain that with an apology.

"All right, are there any questions you have for me, or can I ask mine?"

"For now."

"Go ahead, shoot. We owe you."

It's still baffled me that the first man I interacted with, Arthur was sitting across from me. I would've thought he would've taken off as soon as I told them they were free to run.

"We don't owe him anything."

That was the girl who joined us. I didn't know much about her. She never gave me a name just started talking to me fully when we entered the coffee shop. I didn't know Arthur's son's name either, but he didn't want to tell me. I understood his need to not tell me. I didn't want to know the kid's name — didn't need another thing to feel guilty about. I didn't want to know these people.

I couldn't get to know these people.

I tilted my head, brows furrowed. "So… why kidnap and sell you? Why any of you?"

"You don't know?"

I blinked. "Obviously, I don't know why, hence, I'm asking why!"

Another voice cut in before she could respond again, more measured. "Don't mind her. We're just… confused. The way you handled those guards—we figured you were like us."

I let out a dry laugh. "I don't know about you, but I don't think we're the same at all."

"Well, you aren't human, right?"

I raised a brow. "Wouldn't go that far. I have human attributes, and physically, I am human."

"But you aren't fully human?"

I scanned the group. "Is anyone over here fully human?"

"The Cranes are, and everyone who works for them."

My jaw clenched. Maybe that's why they didn't choose me.

Kidding! They wouldn't be able to tell unless they had access to my medical records to view my genome. No one can get access to that.

"So they are purists? And they what? Kidnap non-humans to sell them for parts or what?"

"Not non-humans," someone corrected softly. "Supernaturals."

"Well, I'll be damned. You don't look supernatural."

"Neither do you."

"That's because I'm not. Not even close."

"Oh? Then what?"

I shook my head "It doesn't matter right now. So why traffic supernaturals?"

"Why else? They hate us, so why not sell us like slaves?"

I ran a hand through my hair, trying to make sense of it. "I don't know. I'm still having trouble understanding why."

I'm, most of the time, not the smartest person. It takes me a while to figure situations out. I'm obviously more brawn than brain — but I do have some smart moments. Today was not one, though.

"They hate us, and they sell us for entertainment."

My stomach turned. "Sell you where and to who?"

I felt guilty making them talk about it, but then again, not knowing was driving me insane.

"To the Normalis side," someone said. "The highest bidder gets us, and they do whatever they want."

Oh fuck!

Now, it makes sense.

"They torture, mutilate, make us fight and kill each other. They hate us so much."

It makes sense now.

They weren't just being sold. They were like me.

They were being used because they were different. Probably, getting experimented on too. Being torn apart, physically and mentally. Being used for human's sick, and twisted games. Becoming the scapegoat for the sins of those bastards. They were bound to be just as fucked as me. That was if they were still alive. Wait! That means those dead would never be given their proper rest and the proper burial.

That's one thing I learned from Waverly. Despite her being mostly supernatural, she went down a path of being more human to take care of us. Even though she remained more humanly, she still followed the practices of respecting the deceased and making sure their soul was properly at rest. I think she did this because of what happened to her mom. She was never properly put to rest. The government took her body because they "owned" the DNA that made her special. Grandpa Spencer was furious, and so was most of her family. I couldn't blame them. She wasn't buried in her family's crypt or given the proper ceremony of life — something they traditionally did in Louisiana. The government just took what it wanted.

Humans took what they wanted!

The only positive — but not really — thing to come out of the government's claim was that they couldn't replicate her electrokinetic DNA. No matter how hard they tried. Yet, when Waverly and Katya personally selected the genetics of their three children and didn't want the electrokinetic DNA, somehow, the three of them still got it. The government had no clue what they were doing, and the ability took a deep root in the DNA of Waverly and her family.

I tried to wrap my head around it, the pieces slowly clicking together.

"So they take supernaturals from here, sell them to rich bastards across the sea, and nobody is talking about this?"

"It's not just from around here — it's up north too. Anywhere where the company is-"

Another voice cut in. "Wherever the company building is on the land they claim for "development", that's where most of the people go missing."

I clenched my jaw. "And nobody asks questions?"

"I'm sure that some people do as well as all those whose family members were taken. Crane Industries cover their tracks well."

"So anyone who dared to talk or question them ended up missing too?"

"Or severely hurt to the point they couldn't even talk," she added quietly.

That made my stomach turn. "How do you know all of this?"

The girl looked up at me—calm but hollow. "You learn a lot under lock and key"

"They tell you this stuff willingly?" She gave a bitter smile.

"Of course not, but the rooms aren't soundproof. You hear a lot when you're isolated." And damn... she was right.

The number of things I overheard at the facility, not that they even cared if we heard their plans. It was just new ways to torture us. Or, as they liked to say, "expand our abilities". Yeah, right!

I scoffed under my breath. "I get it. I really do."

The girl gave me a flat look. "I'm sure."

I didn't like this girl's attitude, but I could see where she was coming from. I was still a stranger, and it didn't matter if I helped them or not.

I could see myself in this girl. Almost like Nova reminded me of -

No!

Stop!

You can't think of her!

You promised you wouldn't when you left!

You fucking promised!

Don't do it!

Don't you fucking dare!

If you walk out that door, forget me! Never think of me again! Don't even try to remember me!

If you're going to treat me like nothing, to go back on your promise, then I'm going to be nothing! I'm no one to you, if you leave!

"Are you okay, buddy?"

"Yeah, you look like you saw a ghost."

I blinked. My throat was tight. "It's nothing. I'm fine. Just processing everything."

"Does it bring up bad memories?"

I nodded slowly. "In a way, yes. But still, our situations are different."

"You're saying you've been through this before?"

"Similar but not the exact same."

I was born — made — to be a killer. They were being sold to be killed.

I was a child being traumatized. They were mostly adults. Minus the kid that is across from me.

I'm not saying we are competing, but I'm sure you could see who had it worse.

It's not a competition, Sean.

I shook the thought away and stood up. "Anyway, I have no more questions, plus I'm done here. I suggest the three of you are too."

One of them glanced at the others nervously. "Where should we go? They'll be looking for us."

"Do you have a car?"

"I do, but they could easily run my plate and track me."

I shrugged. "We'll just have to change a plate then. Switch it with someone who has the same car as you."

I gave her a flat look. "That's illegal!"

I leaned in slightly. "Well, you can either be illegal or end up caught and sold to death. Your choice."

It's obvious what her choice was.

"Where would we go? Where would be safe?"

I tried to soften my tone. Really, I did. "Don't take offense to this- "I paused, trying to be as kind as possible, then added "-you're idiots."

Okay, I said I was trying.

"Excuse us?" The girl snapped.

"What kind of supernaturals are you that you don't even know where to go for safety?"

"Well-"

"Dudes, even I know, and I'm not even one of them!"

Granted, I am adoptively related to the one who rules the safe haven, but still, I never actually met the girl.

"Ok, smartass, where do we go?"

"Fort Oaken, of course!"

After some much-needed direction and thievery, I sent them on their way. It would take them around a day and a half to get there in about another day to get to the capital. At least they'd be safe as soon as they were past the boundaries of Fort Oaken. From there, they could ignore my advice on going to the capital and could just start a new life.

As long as they were safe, that's what really mattered.

I wish I could've done the same for Nova.

At least I helped a few people and got answers. Still, it didn't make sense what was Crane's motive? Why do all of this?

It's not like supernaturals just popped up magically all over the world. They've been an equal part of society since the start of the 22nd century and have been around just as long as humans — just a lot more hidden. So why do this?

Why hunt them?

Why sell them?

Why build an empire on blood?

Sooner or later someone with immense power was going to find out and would destroy Crane Industries. So why? Why not just move over to Normalis and live with their hatred of supernaturals over there? Why did they have to be here? Why did they have to be so cruel to all those people?

That's what they were — people! Just like anyone else.

It was aggravating!

They weren't just supernaturals. They were beings with emotions, feelings, thoughts, and connections to the world just like anyone else.

Fuck!

They were just like anyone else.

So why the fuck Crane Industries?

Why do this?

What the actual fuck!

Why Crane Industries? Why?

It was so frustrating!

I had so many questions. I wanted answers.

No!

Scratch that!

I needed answers!

But the answers I needed couldn't be provided by Arthur or the girl. They had to come from within.

Waverly had better get me those answers soon or else someone would.

From what I was feeling now, I could tear apart the building and everyone inside just to get those answers.

Then something caught my eye. A shadow. Movement. Oh? Well, that was interesting.

A figure hiding on the fire escape. Better yet — just outside my window.

A wicked smirk curled at the corner of my mouth as I stood. Of course, it was him. Who else would be arrogant enough to sneak into my place unannounced?

It could only be one person doing such a thing.

Damien fucking Crane!

In the flesh. In my apartment.

It was my lucky day. Fucking lucky day!

Fuck me!

For once, fate was on my side, and I wasn't going to let that go.

Oh, Damien! Wrong place to be.

Wrong person to fuck with!

Oh, this was going to be good.

But first getting rid of the pest by my window.

Sorry dude, this had to happen.

Damien Crane had to be alone!

Kill him.

Kill him, Sean!

Bleed him like a pig!

Gut him like a pig!

They're all pigs!

Kill them all!

Do it!

Fucking do it!

I steadied my breath. Time to play this right.

He stepped through the threshold that lead to the living room like he owned the place, calm and smug. That signature Crane charm—slicked back and full of shit.

"Do you know it's illegal to break into someone's apartment?" I asked casually, cracking my neck. He didn't flinch.

"Almost as legal as assaulting three men and stealing property." I narrowed my eyes.

Property? Did he mean the people?

"I don't know what you're talking about."

"I'm sure you don't. I'm sure your alibi and lawyer will be good."

"Why would I need either? I did nothing wrong."

He paced slowly, surveying the room. "You know, it's a shame. You wasting your talents on the wrong people. You took down three men and didn't even have a scratch."

"Too bad you passed me on the job."

"Well," he said with a cool shrug, "I needed someone I could trust to protect me."

I scoffed. "No, you wanted a killer. How's that working out for you?"

His grin didn't falter. "He's good. Proven himself quite resourceful, especially when it comes to threats."

Why was he silent?

Why was he pausing?

"I said — especially when it comes to threats."

Another dramatic break?

Oh, wait.

Was he waiting for something?

Oh, right!

I glanced toward the window, then back to him. "Are you trying to get the guy on the fire escape's attention?"

It was oddly satisfying, watching Damien's face twist in confusion and then worry. He also seemed to pale.

"I hope he wasn't the one you wanted to make the dramatic entrance."

Still silence from the once confident man.

"I kind of threw him off beforehand. You know, off the fire escape. He is probably, or I guess hopefully, on his way to the hospital. That or he's dead because, let's be honest, not many people come down this alley."

I could've sworn his face got whiter, and not to toot my own horn, but he looked like he was about to shit himself.

"Not much of a talker now? That's too bad." I leaned in slightly.

"Wh-why?" he finally choked out.

I tilted my head. "Because it means you'll end up being a screamer when I torture you."

"What?!?"

"What what? I thought what I said was clear."

He blinked. Trying to recover his swagger. "Do you not know who I am?"

Awe. Poor guy. There it was. The classic bravado-turned-fear.

He was trying to act confident. He was trying to scare me.

"Damien fucking Crane, the arrogant prick who asked me if I'd kill for him."

I stepped closer, voice like ice. "I guess I lied during that interview. I would kill for you, just not the way you'd expect."

His lip twitched. His voice wavered. "What do-what do you want?"

I didn't blink. "I want to know everything, starting from who your buyers are and ending with the justice that is deserved." I took a breath, slow and deliberate.

His voice cracked. "Why? What justice?"

"Oh my God! You're one of them! You're fucking one of them!"

"I'm one of who?"

His face twisted with disgust. "Those disgusting things!"

And then—he spit at me. Seriously?

"Did you just spit at me?"

I let out a dry laugh. "Wow, that's mature."

I stepped forward, close enough to feel him flinch. "Oh no! Damien Crane," I smiled, slow and cold. "I'm way worse."

He swallowed hard. I leaned in, voice a whisper now, venom laced in every word.

"I'm your lethal consequence!"

FATAL SECRETS

I wouldn't say that kidnapping Damien Crane was my smartest, nor best, idea, however, it was definitely the most beneficial one. I probably wasn't the first person who wanted to kidnap this fucker and interrogate him, but I'd still like to think that I'd go down in the history books for this. Not every day someone kidnaps the son of a powerful company and doesn't get caught right away — or killed. Not that I planned on either of those happening.

Eventually, I would let someone know of my location with this bastard, but now wasn't the time.

Now I know that kidnapping people is the trend at this time because everyone who wants money, kidnaps someone. This wasn't what I was doing. I wasn't trying to follow the trend.

I just wanted answers!

At least I had a goal in mind, unlike all those other people who met their untimely demise by kidnapping the wrong person. Well, that's what happened to those people who took Waverly's sister. Sure, they had a goal. They wanted power, money, anything they could get for returning her alive. I was told people would pay handsomely for her. Yet, they didn't get what they initially thought.

What did they get instead? You may be thinking. Their throats were torn out by the one they took. People shouldn't mess with unstable supernaturals, or that's what they'll get. Plus, if I'm not mistaken, those poor men still rot in that place. The irony.

I guess that's what happens with most kidnappers. But let's be honest now, I wasn't like most. I knew what my goal was, and in the end, if I didn't feel like keeping Damien alive, I wouldn't. I wasn't holding him for ransom or anything. I just wanted to know everything about him and his father's stupid company.

And I don't think that anyone would really know it was me.

I could just kill him right now. Get it over with.

Then I wouldn't get the answers.

Kill him!

Kill the prick now!

No one would know it was me.

Shit!

Well, actually, about that.

The pest on the fire escape. The one who I kept alive.

Of course, I didn't kill him!

It wasn't his fault that he was forced to be there. To work for that twisted company! I wasn't about to kill a man for his poor decisions. I'd leave fate to decide that for him.

But fate was going to come in the form of Mr. Crane.

The poor guy would have to report everything to Mr. Crane and especially tell him about his son's fucked up. He'd report that somehow little ol' me bested both of them and now had Damien captive. So, of course, I left the guy alive.

Who else would tell Crane that it was all me?

Out of the two of them — Damien and the pest — someone had to warn the boss and crew. Out of both of them, one was way more important than the other. It was an easy choice as to who the informant would be.

I almost felt bad.

The poor guy.

Poor little pest!

There was no way Mr. Crane would let him live after letting his son get taken.

The poor, poor guy.

I wanted to feel bad for him.

The key word is WANTED.

Better for Crane to kill his own men rather than any more supernaturals.

It made me wonder how much blood was on his hands, whether that was indirectly or directly. I figured he probably had more indirect blood on his hands. But that was just a guess, I didn't actually know.

Maybe if I saw him, I'd know.

It takes a killer to spot a killer.

But only if he's taken a life with his own hands.

We all had the same dullness in our eyes. That's how you could tell.

Now if it wasn't obvious enough, I lied to Damien Crane. I needed to instill fear in him, and one way of doing that was to make the person feel like they were utterly alone. Well, alone with an insane person.

It was honestly one of my favorite ways of tormenting someone, even if they didn't show fear in their features or instantly crack under pressure. Subconsciously, they would feel the need to run and preserve themselves from me, so one way or another, they would break.

However, to really hammer the nail into their fear, I would leave them alone for some time, but occasionally would make loud noises — whether that was the sharpening of tools or playing with a drill — it would keep their hearts pumping. By the time I actually came in to torture them, they were more than willing to disclose anything to me. That or they would pay me anything to stop and let them go.

I never did.

I couldn't.

No matter how much they paid me, their competitors always paid more.

Then they'd end up dead.

By my hands. My overly bloody hands.

But yes, that's normally how the torment and torture went.

Let's be honest, this time, it wasn't going to run as smoothly as it normally did. I could tell Damien fucking Crane was going to be a handful and wouldn't give me the answers I needed.

There was something about him that was different — other than the fact that this guy was fucking psychotic already. Even when his eyes screamed with fear, his stupid physicality and posture still oozed confidence. It made it apparent that this wasn't his first kidnapping.

But this time?

He wasn't dealing with amateurs.

He was dealing with me.

And I didn't come to play.

I came prepared. It was almost unsurprising that this wasn't his first kidnapping. Obviously, if you mess with certain supernaturals, some — if not all — tend to respond with similar violence back. Leave it to the vampires and wolves to be the messiest when it comes to such things. But judging by the lack of physical scars and still having all his limbs, those poor creatures didn't get far with their torture of Damien. My best guess was they were killed as soon as the rescue team came for the bastard or gassed and then later sold to be killed.

That wasn't going to happen today.

No! Not this time!

I was educated in this type of thing!

They weren't going to find Damien fucking Crane until I wanted them to!

He wouldn't be let go until I had the answers.

I needed those answers!

Of course, when I entered the dark room, I kept him in, mister prick had that stupid, arrogant, and smug look plastered on his fucking face. Like he wasn't tied to a chair.

I wanted to punch it clean off.

I wish I could just punch him!

Oh! Wait now!

He wasn't my boss. He wasn't anyone I associated with.

I just had to pull my punch, so I didn't do too much damage, you know, like accidentally kill the bastard.

What the shit! His face twisted into that same self-important smirk.

Gross!

Why was he bleeding so much?

I didn't even hit him that hard!

Where'd it even come from?

Seriously!

Dude!

Disgusting!

But why did the punch make him worse? Why was he laughing?

What the actual fuck!

How did it make things this much worse?

He spit out some teeth and continued to laugh.

Psycho!

The blood coated the few front teeth he had left.

The sight was straight out of a horror movie.

Damien fucking Crane was psychotic!

I took a step back, fists still twitching.

"Okay! Enough!" I snapped.

He tilted his head, calm as ever—eyes gleaming with something between madness and amusement. "Calm yourself."

"Says the one who punched me!" He grinned, still bleeding. "Seems like you have some anger you want to get out."

I hated him!

Yet…I had to give him credit.

I could applaud his strength. I've met too many people who would cave at the idea or mention of pain. There are too many people who would. It was almost refreshing to have someone different, even a whispered threat can send them into sobbing fits. I was excited to break down his confidence. It would be sickly satisfying to instill fear into this man — especially after all he's done. All his family has done.

Nothing I was planning to do to him would be worse than what they had done.

Sure, I wasn't planning on letting him leave here alive, but at least I wasn't selling him to be mutilated or forced to fight to the death. Killing him would be a mercy.

Maybe I needed to rethink my plan. Or…maybe not.

Either way, breaking Damien fucking Crane would be fun!

It's moments like these that I'm glad I never had a weak stomach, especially with how my brain was formulating the torture I wanted. This might just be the best work I've done. Nevertheless, none of the child assassins were allowed to have weak stomachs — that was one of the first things they worked on with us. They couldn't have any of us throwing up after disfiguring or mutilating our assignments. It wouldn't look good in the confirmation pictures, plus it would leave DNA on the victim. We really couldn't have that happening!

It's safe to say I couldn't afford to have a weak stomach.

In which case, I was glad. I wanted to enjoy the pain I was going to inflict on the bastard.

Damien fucking Crane was just like all those discriminatory assholes in the government! They only cared about the survival of one being — fucking humans! They couldn't be bothered with supernaturals or human experiments. We were nothing to them. An easy dismissal in their eyes.

We shouldn't have been dismissed!

We would be their worst nightmares!

We were their nightmares!

They deserved all the pain they inflicted on us!

Damien fucking Crane deserved this!

"So you kidnap rich guys to ransom money or what?" I blinked slowly.

"You aren't rich, your dad is."

He scoffed. "So you want my dad's money?"

"No!"

Why would I want his blood money?

Seriously!

Why was money the first thing anyone thought of?

I didn't want their fucking money!

I fucking told him what I wanted!

"I want answers to why you do what you do!"

He snorted. "Oh, right, because you want to be a little hero?"

If I had canines like the wolves, I would have snapped them at him.

"I'm not a fucking hero!"

How many times did I have to tell people?

"Of course you aren't. Not even a hero would do something as stupid as you did. I mean, seriously? Kidnapping me? That's your plan! So stupid!"

Quite a stupid boy, Sean?
Shut up!
Shut your fucking mouth!

"How is it stupid to help people?" I snapped.

His smile twisted. "They aren't people. They're beasts! Monsters, if you will!"

My fist made contact with his nose before I could even process it. The sound was solid. His head snapped back.

How dare he!

"What the fuck! What's your problem!"

This time his nose spurted blood. Maybe the next punch would be followed by a satisfying crunch.

That is wishful thinking, though.

"The only monster I see is YOU!"

The fucking prick with no empathy for people struggling!

He deserved this!

Kill him!

Kill him!

"How could I forget?" he croaked, grinning through the blood. "You're a lover of them! Why else would you help them?"

I wasn't a lover of them! I just had respect for them. I had to!

Waverly gave me a life. She let me have a name and become a person rather than a machine. I owed her everything, and I owed her family everything!

And this bastard!

Damien fucking Crane!

He was killing off her kind — her family — and not even batting an eye with care or empathy.

Those poor people didn't deserve this. They didn't deserve to be taken from their families and forced over to a place that despised them. Nobody should have to deal with that!

Damien fucking Crane!

His fucking father!

Their fucking company!

They were doing this to those beings. Why!
What did they ever do to the Cranes?
Why do this?

Fuck!
I wanted him dead!
I wanted him fucking dead!
Kill him!
Gut him like the pig he is!
Kill him!

I clenched my fists tighter—held back, just barely.

"I'm stopping them from being traumatized! From having a fate worse than death!"

He scoffed, eyes gleaming with that same twisted pride. "What about all those who they've hurt?"

"What's that supposed to mean? Who have they hurt?"

His smile widened, and my blood boiled. "Society! My family has suffered! Do you know how much land had to be given to those monsters just because it was sacred to them?"

You're fucking kidding me!

"We've lost half our sales because of them! And sometimes people don't want to work because of certain times of the month! Stupid fucking full moon! Nobody wants to work then."

My jaw twitched. My vision blurred with rage.

"Let me get this straight —" I said, voice shaking with rage. "You kidnap and send supernaturals to their deaths because they have claimed their rights?"

He sneered. "It's not their right! We had the land before any of them!"

Of course. Talk about a spoiled prick.

He couldn't have been serious!

There's no way the Cranes were willing to traffic these people just because they were getting equal rights as anyone else.

"So they haven't actually hurt anyone?"

"They have been hurting my family's business!"

What the fuck!

They've been killing these poor people for their business. Their fucking business!

Oh, you have no clue how much I was going to enjoy hurting him now.

That selfish bastard. That stupid fucking prick!

Indirectly killing people because they lost a little bit of business.

You had to fucking kidding me!

Pathetic!

Pathetic wastes of air.

I turned without another word. "Wait! Where are you going? I'm not done."

"You are done talking about that. I still need my answers and I have a feeling you won't disclose them willingly." I didn't look back.

"Damn straight, I'm not snitching!"

Oh, but you already did. Not with intent—but your mouth ran faster than your brain. You'd given me enough to justify what came next. And now?

It was going to be very fun making him squeal.

Gut him like a pig!

Then after he's given all that he knows, I'll consider letting him go.

Who was I kidding? There was no way he was getting out of here alive. I fucking hated him and everything about him, he deserved to die. Then I'd go after the head of the company.

I didn't think that the death of his son would deter Mr. Crane from his business.

They were all psychotic, being the cause of so many supernaturals' demise. They deserved a fate just as bad as the one they gave so many supernaturals.

I'd give all those who were taken and killed the justice they deserved.

They would be put to rest. Proper rest.

I really hated them all! They were twisted and liked playing God just to get some money back. But let's be honest now, it didn't matter how many supernaturals they took and sold, they were never getting the land back. They were never going to be able to.

They'd have to commit an entire genocide to reclaim that land.

Nobody would let them do that.

Then again, I thought no one would let this happen to supernaturals either. Yet, here we are.

Maybe it's time to rethink the whole human government and just let the supernatural one take full control. This wouldn't happen if they took full control. At least, I hope it didn't happen.

I guess I left out one of the main parts of my torture method— the method itself.

It wasn't mine originally. It was something Waverly had designed back in her day as an assassin, but it wasn't a weapon then.

It was a tiny nanobyte.

Barely the size of a grain of sand.

Once embedded under the skin, it did something incredible: It shut off pain. Any kind of pain.

Waverly mainly designed it for people who couldn't handle pain very well when they were healing from wounds. A way to help the weak recover without screaming every time they breathed. But you had to keep the nanobyte embedded in until the healing process of the injury was completely done, whether that was for days or months. Failure to keep it in would cause the person to feel the pain again. Your body would remember everything. Every slice. Every burn. Every shattered bone. All of it—felt tenfold.

That's why it was my method of choice. You could embed the device into someone, shut off all their pain, and then proceed to break every bone in their body. They feel every break, every strain of their muscles, and their nerves being on fire all in seconds. It was the perfect way to torture someone.

It was the perfect way to get information.

It would be the perfect torture tool to get everything I wanted from Damien fucking Crane. And the best part? I wouldn't really have to lift a finger. But I wanted to, I wanted him to feel the full force of my ability.

No more holding back my punches. He'd feel what true power felt like. And that feeling of power would come in the form of searing pain.

I wasn't doing this for vengeance. I was giving him what he deserved!

He deserved this!

He really fucking did!

But of course, before I could re-enter the room with my favorite toy, Waverly had to call. I swore she knew everything about what I was doing—she always knew.

I wonder if that's because I reminded her of herself at this age. Someone willing to fight the bad when everyone else looks the other way. But in her case, the bad came in the form of her sister, someone who manipulated the narrative every chance she got. Someone who always played the victim and blamed whoever was against her. Waverly — my adopted mother — put a stop to that soon after her sister hurt her children. Waverly really loved those kids like her own, of course, that was before she had her own, so it made sense to why she was so devoted to them. But as soon as her sister did that god-awful thing to them, Waverly's back turned against her. She turned everyone against her sister, exposing the true nature of her sister's monster.

I was gonna do the same to Crane Industries. Everyone needed to see the monster that they were. They weren't ridding the world of them like they thought — not that any of those people were monsters — but they were just creating more. They were creating themselves into monsters. And just like Waverly, I had to show the world the true colors of the company. Of that god-awful family!

But as I was saying, Waverly called me. She had news. More information on Crane Industries.

I didn't have to tell her what I had done, because she already knew.

How did she know?

How did she always know?

I swear she was watching me, monitoring me, all the time. Let's be honest that wasn't probably true. She just knew me better than I knew myself. Even if I didn't want her to.

She couldn't know me.

I didn't want her to know me.

I wasn't that young boy she found cowering in the corner of a cell in that facility.

I was never that young boy. It was a façade.

I was always a killer. The machine that was genetically made.

I wasn't human.

And yet she still knew me. She still believed in that young boy even if I didn't. She still had faith that he was somewhere in me.

But only I knew the truth. He was dead as soon as he was birthed into the world.

That little boy never existed.

That innocent boy died before she could get to him. Innocence didn't last long in the hands of monsters. And he died before she could save him.

Her voice pulled me out of the pit. Soft. Familiar. Heavy with sadness. "Oh darling, what are you doing?"

My eyes stayed on the floor—cold and detached. "You already know the answer to that question."

There was a pause. A sigh. "I know, I just wish it wasn't true. I just wish you would've talked to me before, darling."

I clenched my jaw, trying to stay level. "There wasn't much talking to be done. He broke into my apartment, and I acted off that. End of discussion."

She exhaled again, slower this time, letting it go. "I see. Well, I have the information for you, I think you would find it rather… enlightening."

A flicker of tension loosened in my shoulders. "I'm all ears, it's not like the bastard is going anywhere."

"Be nice," she said gently. I let out a hollow laugh.

"It's difficult, especially after all I've learned from him. He comes from a family of sick and twisted psychos. You'd agree with me if you heard what he was saying."

"I'm sure I would," she said quietly. "But still, I don't want you to feed into his insanity. He'll feed off your anger, and that —" her voice firmed "——will leave you vulnerable. You need to be smart about this."

I nodded, more to myself than to her. "I know. I am being smart."

"Good," she replied, calm but cautious. "Now for this information, I've sent it to your hard drive, but also the system in your phone. You know that one I installed for you years ago."

"Great, so I can access it now."

I crossed the room and picked up my other phone, flicking the screen on. "Yes, but be careful," she warned. "This information is hard to come by, and you don't want it to get into the wrong hands. You don't want people to know that you have it either."

"I know the drill," I muttered, already opening the file. "Don't worry everything will be safe and encrypted as soon as I'm done going over it."

That was one of the benefits of the software that Waverly designed for my phone, well, all her children's phones. We were able to encrypt messages and put a code on them so that no one, not even the government, could have access to them. Only those with the specific genetic access codes could read what was otherwise a jumbled mess of illegible data. I guess that's a perk to having a mother with the ability of electrokinetic DNA, even if she wasn't my biological mother. Plus, she was too smart for her own good. I bet the government was lucky to have her on their side in the beginning, now she could care less if they needed her help or anything. The only reason she worked so vigilantly for them was to get the assassin program shut down — the child program, if you want to say. As soon as that program was done, she no longer needed to answer them. They no longer had leverage over her.

I'm surprised she hadn't taken over the government by now. She hated the human government just as much as the rest of us do.

"Would you please just be careful? Can you promise me that?"

She really did care for us — for me.

And I was a disappointment, always letting her down. Always doing the wrong thing.

Why did she have to care so much?

Why did she have to be so motherly?

Why couldn't she just hate me?

"Yeah, I can try."

"Darling. I need you to be safe. I'd tear apart the whole world if anything happened to you."

I wanted to believe what she said. I really wanted to believe. But there's no way she could care this much about me.

I wasn't even biologically hers.

I was not her son.

She didn't know me.

Not the real me.

"Thanks, I'll contact you soon for any of the updates."

"Please stay safe, darling. I love you."

Click. The line went dead. Just like my ability to respond. I never said it back. I don't think I had ever said it back. Maybe once, when I was a child, but I couldn't be too sure.

I think deep down I loved her too. She was the woman who raised me as her own. And on paper, legally I was her child. We share the same last name. So yeah, probably deep down I loved her too. But I would never say it back.

I could never say it back.

She didn't know me enough for me to say it.

Plus, I hated myself too much to ever really believe that someone loved me.

Why would anyone ever love me? I mean truly love me.

I was a killer and a monster. Nothing more.

So no one would love me, and I didn't blame them.

Damien fucking Crane was waiting for me. And seeming as I made him wait so long, it was back to my torturing I go. I was going to have fun getting all the information. Enjoy watching that smug look slip off his face.

"Took you long enough to get your ass back here."

There it was. That same shit-eating grin. Smug. Arrogant. I couldn't wait to wipe it off his face. Not for long, I thought.

"What took you so long? I was getting bored waiting." I stepped forward, slowly. Letting my silence speak first.

"I had other business to attend to. You're not the only one I'm getting my information from."

He tilted his head. Smirk growing. Like he knew something I didn't. "Oh yeah, like your mom."

My heart stopped. "What?"

"Your mother, Waverly Barnes."

What the fuck!

Oh no! Oh no! No! No!

No!

Fuck!

"You see, you're not the only one who can get information." My fists clenched. My blood ran ice cold. I could feel the air shifted around me.

"How did you get it? When did you get it?" He said it so casually. So matter-of-fact. Like it wasn't a grenade tossed into my sanity.

"Before I got to your apartment. My dad had done some digging of his own when he saw the last name 'Barnes' pop up in our list of applicants."

Fuck! My breathing picked up. I was trying to stay calm — to keep myself from snapping.

As much as our medical records and full birth certificate – meaning our abilities – were sealed, it was still public who the Barnes were. Grandpa Spencer was an old veteran of the Cold War. He was one of the first genetically modified humans – thanks to the work of a crazy scientist. And my adopted mother, Waverly Barnes was known throughout the world as the woman who fought for the closure of human experimental facilities. Not to mention the assassin company that she created, which included the protection of vigilantes, superheroes, and assassin's identities. She also helped develop many technologies with the Knight Corporation. That company aided in her development of the circuited clothing that she had us wear, as well as the nanobytes for helping people heal painlessly.

It wasn't hard to do research on those two.

As for me and my adoptive siblings, all of our records were sealed. The only things being our adoption certificates and the people who took us in. Nothing about our enhanced genetics or previous employment was allowed for the public eye, nor the government's. Only specific people with a specific amount of clearance were allowed access to that, and even then, the access was limited.

So how much did this fucker really know?

"So you know my mom, whoop-de-do. A lot of people do." I shrugged. But I could feel the rage burning in my throat.

"I wasn't done," he said, his grin returning like it never left. "I know all about you — well, about your family. Your real family."

He couldn't. Those records were sealed!
He couldn't know!
This was a bluff.
This had to be a bluff!

I tilted my head, keeping my expression blank. "Oh? Okay, sure."

"You know there are many powerful people who support our company and how we make money. People who are in the government. The PROPER government."

"Your point." My jaw tightened. His tone made my skin crawl.

"They gave us some interesting information about who you really were."

Don't react. Don't give him anything. He doesn't know. If he really knew who I was, he wouldn't have broken into my apartment. But I wasn't about to call his bluff. But then he said it.

"Born over in Normalis. Kidnapped by that beast woman, Waverly. Torn from your birth mother's arms. She's still alive, you know." What the fuck. My stomach dropped.

He wasn't bluffing.

Of course, I knew that. But there were so many times that I wish she wasn't. Yet Damien fucking Crane's narrative portrayed an infant being taken — stolen — from its mother into the arms of Waverly. That wasn't the case, the woman who gave birth to me willingly handed me over to the people in the facility. She gave me up to be tortured and tormented at the beginning of my childhood. It was all because she worked with them – she was just like them. One of the monsters in the lab coats. But Waverly saved me, she saved all of us. Waverly took us away from that life, gave us a purpose, and then the government tried to rip it away from us. They force us to have a new purpose, one that we would continue having for many, many years.

Waverly wasn't the monster in my story, every human — every nonpowered human — I ever encountered was.

"Did you know she looks for you?"

What? No!

That wasn't good.

That couldn't be true!

"She looks for you and your sister. Your real sister."

No!

I couldn't!

I couldn't think of her!

"What was her name again? Penelope? Penny?"

He smirked. "Oh, right! Isn't it Pearl?"
No! Fuck!
No! Don't think!
Don't remember her!
Don't think of her!
You promised!
You fucking promised!
I left, and I promised I wouldn't do it!

* * *

*"You're leaving me! Why? What did I do?
You promised to take me with you! You promised! Why
are you breaking it? Why are you leaving me here?
I'm supposed to go with you! You said I would!
Don't you dare leave me! Don't you
dare walk out that door!
If you walk out, don't expect me to care about you
anymore! Don't expect me to answer your calls!
If you walk out that door, forget me! Never think
of me again! Don't even try to remember me!
If you're going to treat me like nothing, to go
back on your promise, then I'm going to be
nothing! I'm no one to you if you leave!
Sean! Don't leave me!
Please don't leave me!"*

* * *

"Did you know your mother would pay a hefty price to get both of you back? Especially little Pearl."
No!

That could only mean trouble. She never wanted anything to do with us when we were near her, and yet as soon as the facility got shut down, she now desperately wanted us back. Ironic.

"You know," Damien continued, voice syrupy with malice, "I like that name Pearl. It sounds so sweet. So innocent. It would be a shame if someone ruined that."

My blood turned to ice. "What did you do?"

He shrugged, tugging uselessly against the restraints. "Oh me? Well, I haven't done anything. I'm tied to the chair. But my father, well, that's a different story."

For fuck's sake.

"Call it leverage or whatever, but he's probably getting her as we speak. You know for an exchange." He grinned like the devil.

"Actually—" he tilted his head smugly, "Originally, I was supposed to kidnap you but obviously… that didn't work out."

Oh my god!

Oh my GOD!

Fuck!

This was not good!

Fuck!

Why didn't I just leave it all alone?

You're so fucking stupid, Sean!

What have you done?

What did you fucking do!

Waverly was gonna kill me.

She was going to kill me!

"Would your father do the exchange?" I hissed, trying to keep my voice level.

Damien smirked. "I think he'd be open to it."

"But how much of you does he need for the deal?" His brows pulled together.

"What do you mean?"

"Can there be parts missing?" My tone was ice. The calm before the storm.

"I… don't understand what you mean."

"What I mean is, I'm gonna rip you apart and make sure you feel every fiber of your body being torn."

"You're going to pay for dragging her into this!"

They were all gonna pay!

How fucking dare they try to bring seventeen-year-old child into this?

She was a child!

What the fuck is wrong with them!

They all had to pay for this!

And Damien fucking Crane would be the first!

DEADLY GAME

I was incredibly screwed! Waverly warned me to be safe, but now that was out of the question. Pearl was in danger, and I was willing to do anything to get her out.

I really fucked up this time!

Such a stupid man, Sean!

I had really gone and done it now. I didn't know how I could fix it. How the hell was I supposed to fix this?

Could I even fix this? Could I even save her?

I mean, I tried to help Nova and look where that landed me—sitting in a storm I created, dragging my family into it.

I'm such a fucking idiot!

Why did I have to get involved? Why did I even bother with any of this?

All because I thought I could do something right for once.

I should have left everything alone. I should have forgotten about the encounter with Nova.

I should have never applied at Crane Industries!

I'm such a fuck up!

Stupid boy!
Stupid!
Stupid!
Stupid!

At least I could say I did one thing right—planting that nanobyte into the nape of Damien's neck and waiting for it to take full effect. He was going to feel my full strength and the pain that he caused others. Maybe when I was done with him, I would show mercy — not that he deserved it. Not that any of them deserved it!

But I couldn't stay in the room as the nanobyte worked its way into his nervous system. I was too eager to destroy him that I knew I wouldn't have let it take its full effect before ruining him. I took the time away from him to try and get a hold of Bexley. My older adopted sister would be the last person to be with Pearl, so I had to warn her that someone was coming.

I hit call.

Hi, you reached the voicemail of—

Shit!

Why wouldn't she answer?

This was important!

She knew it was my number!

Why won't she answer?

I hit redial.

Hi, you reached the voicemail of—

Again? Really?

What could she be doing?

Fuck!

Who else would be with Pearl?

I mean, she lived in Florida with Bexley, but who was still around there? I know a few of us live under Bex's roof as we finished high school after the program was shut down, but that was years ago. Chances are, everyone left like I did. I didn't really know who would be around there anymore, other than Bex.

Hi, you reached the voicemail of—

Fuck!

Why couldn't she just answer?

Who else would I call? Who else could I call?

Fuck!

I just wanted to know if she was okay. I just wanted to get her away from danger by giving her a heads-up.

Maybe I should just call her number.

I know I told her I would never call, but this was important. Her life was at stake. I was just trying to protect her. I hit the call button. Held my breath.

"Come on, sis, just answer the phone."

Just answer the phone and yell at me. At least yelling would make me know that you were alright.

Hey! Sorry I couldn't-

"Hello?"

Thank fuck!

"Pearl! Whatever you do, don't hang up. It's me, Sean. I know I shouldn't have called, but I need to tell you something really quick. You're in danger! You need to get away from wherever you are right now—"

Her voice cut in. "Oh hey, Dad, what are you doing calling me so late?"

What?

"You know it's a school night, and I'm supposed to be going out with friends tonight." Her laugh — carefree.

"You really need to talk? Okay, I guess I can spare a few minutes." Her tone was light. Carefree. Like nothing was wrong. My stomach turned. This wasn't normal.

"Pearl, are you in danger? Is there someone with you?" I kept my voice low, tight — like I could somehow squeeze the urgency through the phone.

"Yes Dad, I'm doing just fine in school." Her voice was slightly louder, maybe performative. Fuck — this was code. Ok, shit! How was I going to do this? I had to keep going, keep her talking, keep her safe.

"Are they familiar to you?"

"No Dad, it's nobody you know!" There was an emphasis in her denial — forced, deliberate.

"Is there any way you can describe them?" I was fishing, praying she'd drop something, anything I could work with.

"I already told you I wasn't hanging out with the wrong crowd." She acted defensive.

"The people I hang out with though they look big and scary, they're just gentle giants deep down."

Then, a low, stern, and unfamiliar voice cut through the line. "Hurry up, we are going to be late." That did not sound like the voice of a teenage boy. My blood went cold.

"See Dad, that's one of them there." She sounded calm, but I could hear the tension layered beneath.

"Do you know what they want?" I whispered, the words barely getting past my dry lips.

"No, we're just gonna go see a movie." She was trying to keep it together. But I knew better.

"Do you know where they're taking you? Give me something—a clue, a landmark, or anything, Pearl."

"I'm not sure what movie we're seeing." Another answer is vague on purpose. Fuck — they were right there with her.

"Pearl, I need you to listen very closely," I said, trying not to choke on the words. "You need to get out of there! Punch, kick, bite, do whatever you have to to get out."

"Pearl?" Suddenly, the line stayed silent.

"Well, well, well," a new voice drawled, "You sound a little too young to be a dad."

Fuck!

"So, who do I have the pleasure of speaking to then?" His tone was mock-friendly — the kind that made your skin crawl.

"Fuck you!" I snapped. No time for games.

"Don't tell me!" he said in a voice soaked with sarcasm. "Are you Sean Barnes?" I could hear the grin through the phone.

"Are you the father of the bastard I'm about to torture?" My heart pounded like a warning drum.

"Well, it's nice to meet you too, Sean. I was just about to wonder where my son was with you, but I guess you got to him first."

"You don't sound too surprised?" I spat, barely holding it together.

"Well, as much as I was looking forward to this little family reunion between you and your dear little sister, I know the kind of fuck up my son is. He's too cocky for his own good." He laughed, casually — like this was just business.

"And yet you sent him to get me with only one bodyguard for protection?" I was stalling, trying to buy time while my mind raced.

"I didn't know who I was fully dealing with," he said slowly. "Not until your little sister decided to blow a hole through one of my men's sternums. It now makes sense why your dearest mother wants you back. You're both very special." My heart stopped.

"We're not special, you giant rat-faced ahh—" The insult burst out in the background of our call.

"Don't you fucking hurt her!" I roared, stepping forward like I could reach through the phone.

"And what are you going to do?" he sneered. "You're thousands of miles from here, you can't protect her."

<hr>

"What do you think you're going to do? You go out there, ready to punch everything — everyone — in your path. That's not how things work anymore. You can't just rely on your strength, especially when it comes to raising her. You can't protect her out there. The only way to truly protect her is to leave her behind. That way, you were giving her the best chance of a life, one we could never have."

<hr>

"I may be thousands of miles away, but the same can be said about your son. Whatever you do to her, I will do to him tenfold."

A pause.

"So what are you thinking? A little exchange?" he said mockingly. "My son for your little sister?"

"I don't see it any other way."

"Hmm. Or…" he sounded too calm. "Well, I could hand her over to your mother, send my men after you, and get paid either way. Sounds like a win-win to me."

"Your son would be dead in seconds. And nothing you'd do would ever make up for that. Because in the end, we'll get out and come back to destroy you."

"I personally do not want to be destroyed." His smugness slipped just a little. "So let's say we trade—my son for your sister. Are you saying you'd stop interfering? Walk away and leave my business alone?"

My thoughts were spinning. Damn it. If I said yes, I'd be turning my back on Nova and everyone else trapped in his system. But if I said no… Pearl would be gone. Forever.

But I ended up with no choice, "Yes."

"No more interfering with my business."

Fuck!

I wouldn't be able to help Nova.

But am I really helping her now?

All I've managed to do in these past few hours — these few days — is fuck things up again. Why couldn't I just leave everything well enough alone? Why did I feel so gung-ho about helping someone? Why couldn't I just keep my nose out of other people's business?

Look where this has all gotten me. I have the son of a worldwide supernatural trafficker locked in a room behind me. Meanwhile, said supernatural trafficker is currently at my sister's house holding her hostage. And I'm not even a step closer to helping Nova.

Maybe it was for the best that I gave up.

Help Pearl and turn my focus elsewhere. Eventually, I would forget about this whole ordeal, this whole trafficking mess.

That's what it was for the best. That's what would make sure Pearl stayed out of our mother's clutches.

That's how it should've been done.

"Yes. I'll leave you to your business."

"Wonderful. I'll send you a location where we can exchange."

"Hold up-" I cut in instinctively.

That was rather abrupt.

I didn't like it. I didn't trust him. Yet for the sake of Pearl, I would follow through with my promise. No more being involved with this business.

I needed to put Nova behind me. Put all of them behind me.

For the sake of Pearl.

The heavy door creaked as I stepped back into the dimly lit room. "Back again for more fun?" Damien's voice was smooth, cocky, like he hadn't spent the last hour strapped to a chair. His smirk flickered beneath the bruises.

I didn't flinch. "More like I want answers."

He gave an exaggerated sigh, rolling his head against the back of the chair. "Again? I thought we were over this, and I thought you got your answers from your mom."

I crossed the room slowly, my footsteps deliberate. "She can only get so much information. I want an insider's knowledge."

Damien's grin stretched wider, defiant. "How very demanding of you." He leaned forward as much as the restraints would allow. "Except, as I said, I'm not going to squeal."

That's what he thought.

"That's okay," I said, tone almost casual. "I'll wait for that part, but first, tell me about your father. He wants to meet to do an exchange."

Damien tilted his head lazily, eyes narrowing. "What do you want me to tell you?"

"I want to know if it's safe that he won't backstab me."

He smirked, ever the smug bastard. "What if I lie to you? How will you know?"

"Trust me…" I stepped closer, my voice low. "You won't want to lie."

His smirk twitched. "You should meet him, it's completely safe."

Despite what he said, his actions showed otherwise. He looked fearfully expecting some sort of pain to shoot through him as he lied. When nothing happened, he began to laugh, shoulders loosening as he'd just won something.

"Some great technology you got there," he muttered. "Barely does it's job."

I smiled — and it wasn't friendly. "Trust me, it's doing its work perfectly."

I let the silence stretch and watched the tension crawl up his neck. "Now," I said, voice sharper, "You wanna try and answer my question again truthfully?"

His lips parted. "If you meet him, everything will go exactly as you expect."

It's cryptic, but technically, it's not a lie. I was expecting to show up and have more than a dozen men surrounding me and incapacitating me. But of course, Damien fucking Crane would never tell me that to my face. Instead, I did the next best thing.

During the little nap I gave Damien while transporting him to this location, I prepped the room. I put an assortment of tools to help me with my interrogation and torment of him. Obviously, I wasn't going to torture this guy without tools.

The first ones grabbed were something I had previously avoided using. I'm not sure why, but I just did. The tools were ten nails and a hammer. I had only seen one other person attempt this method, so I made no promises that it would be done perfectly.

"Ooooh," he cooed, his voice mocking. "What are you going to do with those?"

Why bother telling him when I could just show him?

I placed the extra nails in my mouth, as I aligned a singular one to the tip of his finger. The idea was to embed the nail under his fingernails. Supposedly there were a lot of nerves around that area, and it hurt like a bitch when they were ripped out after.

There I went, nailing each of the ten under his nail bed and watching Damien's face shifted from one of horror to one of confusion. He seemed utterly speechless from the lack of pain he was feeling, but that wouldn't last for very much longer. My attention adjusted back to the nanobyte, as I place my hand on the back of his neck to rip it out.

"What's his plan for when I meet him?" I asked, my voice cold.

"I really told you, I'm not ughahh-"

His scream tore through the room, echoing off the walls like a breaking siren. His body jerked against the restraints, the pain hitting harder and faster than expected. Usually, it took a minute or two for the nerves to recalibrate. Not this time. Damien wasn't like the others who were under the effects of the nanobyte. It was almost like his nerves were already aware of what might happen. The nail technique must've worked better than I thought.

I tilted my head. "Do you want to answer the question or not?"

"Screw- screw you!" he spat; his jaw clenched through the agony.

I guess not. Time to start getting answers. I ripped the first nail out.

Of course, he screamed.

"What's your father's plan!" I asked again.

"I'm not- I'm not telling you!" he panted.

There goes the second.

"I still have eight more to go and a bunch of other methods I can get answers," I said calmly, "but we could run this quickly, and you could just answer the question now."

His glare said everything. "I'm not talk- talking."

"Fine! Have it your way!"

He seemed to brace himself for another nail being ripped out, but I did the opposite. I pushed the second nail straight back into his finger. Only this time, pushing it so far, it began to split his fingernail in two.

I know I used to hate the sound coming from previous assignments and the pain I was inflicting on them, but right now, Damien's cries are almost satisfying. Maybe it's because he actually deserved the pain I was inflicting? Or maybe because after all these years my past had finally caught up, and I was just a twisted motherfucker. Who really knew?

"Hold up!" Damien gasped for breath "I'll start talking. Just give me a second."

I had barely grabbed the nail I had replaced, and he was already willing to open up to me. I gave him a beat and expected him to start spewing as much information as he could.

Of course, that's not what he actually ended up doing. Instead, he spit on me, and I ripped two nails out.

His scream was raw, jagged—like metal scraping against metal. "Fuck!"

"Keep it up!" I snapped, wiping my face. "This will only get worse! This is the tamest method that I'll be trying today!"

"He will do the exchange." His chest rose like it was being punched from the inside.

Fourth one out.

"Stop lying to me!"

"I'm not," he cried. "He won't hurt you if you have me with you."

One hand done. One more to go. Then, we go onto a more exciting method.

"Okay! He might be planning a trap!"

I stopped. It was almost like a programming: he gives me a wrong answer, and I take one out. He gives me a right answer, I give him a break — well a break from the instant pain, not the lingering one underneath his fingernails.

"I don't know what exactly," Damien stammered, "but there's a chance it's a setup."

"Keep going," I ordered, my voice low and even.

"I told you I don't know!"

And there goes the next nail.

He shrieked, body jerking against the restraints. "What's your- your problem? I said I don't know!"

Three left. Then the next tool comes out.

"Okay, okay!" he gasped. "I have an idea of what might happen! Just hold on!"

I think he was trying to calm his heart. He was taking rather deep breaths.

"I told you that your mother is looking for you," he continued, his words shaking. "Well, he still might— might try to sell you both to her."

My hands clenched. "Would there be any way for me to change the location, like suggest a new one?" I asked.

His laughter seemed rather forced and weak. "Are you joking? There is no way my father would meet up with you at a location of your choice. He would never trust it."

And yet he expected me to trust his location. Seems quite hypocritical if you ask me.

"So even if I made a promise to stay out of his business' way, he'll still turn on me."

"Well yeah, unless he can legally get you to sign a waiver saying you won't get involved there's no way for him to know whether or not your promise means shit."

Fantastic!

"What kind of location would he suggest?"

"How am I supposed to know, we have a bunch of locations that we own."

Damien was getting too cocky — too comfortable, I had to remind him of the position he was in. Eight down, two more!

"Jesus fuc-"

"Told you I didn't know."

"Think harder!" I warned. "Or else the next one comes out! Or maybe another goes in?"

I had to keep him on his toes, or else he would be expecting the pain of the nail being ripped out.

Then again, I could completely throw him off by going onto my next tool. That would mean I would have to grab it, though.

It might scare Damien if I start moving around, it would definitely throw him off.

That's what I did, I got up from my place beside him and I went to grab the next tool — a drill and some razor wire.

"Whoa, hold up, buddy!"

I found a somewhat pleasurable instilling fear into him. God, I really was becoming twisted – becoming a monster once again.

"There's a few locations where he might suggest," Damien rushed, desperation creeping in "Chances are it'll be one of these three —" I tilted my head, gesturing for him to continue. "There's an old cabin that we never really visited anymore, which is very secluded and surrounded by the woods. It would make for a perfect opportunity to catch someone off guard and get the upper hand."

The way he said that sounded like it had happened before or numerous times before.

"The next one is a little odd, we have this old, abandoned pipeline warehouse that we were hoping to fix up and develop into mansions or whatever. But we never could do anything because there's still lingering gas from the pipeline in the air, and a demolition crew couldn't get it to properly take down the warehouse."

It sounds like a cool place, but I don't understand why they would keep property if they couldn't even work on it and resell it. It seemed rather odd indeed.

"And the last one, " he paused, eyes flicking to mine, "is a bunch of sea-cans by the docks. This one is a little more obvious than the others, as chances are you will be sold. That's what we use the sea-cans for. To ship those beasts across the ocean."

I don't know what really came over me, but I ripped the next nail out. Maybe I was tired of him being so helpful and not getting the torture he deserved, or maybe I just missed the sound of his agony?

Yep! I was definitely becoming that monster again.

"What- what the shit!"

"I was- wasn't lying."

"I know," I said coolly, "but you're still a prick for kidnapping and selling people!"

"Screw you!"

And there goes the last one. I feel like I didn't spend too much time on this method, but alas all the fun things have to come to an end. At least I got to move on to another method.

"Here, have this, it'll help prepare you for the next best thing."

I pierced the nanobyte back into his neck. The agony that was on his face quickly dissolved as nanobyte began to work its magic. Sure, it didn't take away the pain in the instant, but it helped ease it a bit.

I had to wait now, before continuing on. I wanted him to be numb to what I was about to do next. So, as I waited, I began cutting away his jeans from his mid-thigh. Obviously, it was so I could get better access to his legs.

"What kind of freak are you?" he spat. "Trying to get into my pants!"

Crack

I was serious when I said the next time I punched him, I would end up breaking his nose. Only this time, he couldn't feel the pain, not yet at least. And despite his numbness to the pain, his nose still gushed blood down his face.

"Ha! Didn't even hurt!" he cackled, his teeth slick with blood.

Once again, he got blood in his mouth, and it was disgusting to look at.

Also, I'm not entirely sure if he was the smartest. Did he really not realize that the nanobyte was taking away his sensations of pain? That it was rerouting his pain receptors to ignore the damage being done to his body. How could he not figure that out?

"Who's your biggest seller?" I asked flatly.

Damien threw his head back in prolonged laughter. I took the time to drill one end of the razor wire into his kneecap, but he didn't seem to notice. Because the sound of the drill and the pressure in his knee weren't something he should worry about — totally!

"Are you done with the conversation on my father already?" he sneered.

"No," I said calmly, beginning to drill into the second spot just below the joint, "but I don't really care about that right now. I'm getting the answers I originally wanted."

"Right, right. The whole reason why you took me in the first place."

"Wait! What are you doing?"

It took him long enough to see what I was doing. I had already finished the second drilling of the razor wire into his right knee and now was beginning to wrap it around his calf on both sides.

"Why can't I feel that? What did you do to me!"

Now, he was finally starting to piece things together. Took him long enough. It also started to make sense why he needed a bodyguard and why he needed them to kill. He was completely stupid! Having no sense of survival or a strategy in his brain. Just a cocky little shit with a name and a bank account to hide behind.

"Don't worry, you'll feel it soon enough," I muttered. "Just let me finish up this last wrap."

"Seriously, fucking stop! What did you do!"

He attempted to kick his legs out, but it only made the razor wire dig deeper into the skin.

"Stop moving, or you'll end up killing yourself!"

"Screw you! Let me go! Get these off me!"

It's strange he didn't react when I nailed under his fingertips and yet now, he's reacting. It's almost like now he's realizing the severity of this — the severity of his and his family's actions. These were the consequences!

"If you keep moving, chances are you'll nick a major artery, and you bleed out in seconds."

Somehow, that seemed to stop his kicking but not his screaming.

"You twisted, sick, psychotic bastard!"

"I'm going to fuck you up as soon as I get out!"

"You're going to wish you were ughaahhh-"

There goes the nanobyte again. And it was perfect timing for it to be gone, I was tired of hearing his pathetic comments. Let's be honest, he wasn't getting out of here — well, he wasn't getting out of there alive.

"Who's your biggest seller? I won't ask again!"

I began pulling on the ends of the wire, digging the razors deeper into his calf. They had to be in the right position — in the perfect amount of skin and muscle — in order for this to work properly. Thankfully, with all his kicking a few seconds ago, getting these wires into position would be quicker than I thought.

"Kiss- kiss my ass!" he spat, breathless but still trying to act like he had control.

Why was he getting all cocky again? He did remember the nail technique, right? Did he already forget how quickly he crumbled when I started with the nails? Why was he not making this easier for himself? Sure, I was excited to do this method, but I also just want an answer at this point. Why was he making it so difficult for the both of us?

I clenched my jaw. "Names now!"

"Say- say please."

That was it! Time to show him the rest of this torment!

I grabbed some jumper cables, I had jimmy-rigged into the electrical socket, I placed them on the bottom of the wire. Then, I sat back and watched as he kicked around in pain, pulling the razors deeper into his skin and burning his skin. His back arched. A scream tore out of him.

"Stop! Please stop!"

I detached the cables for a second.

There are many things wrong with me, but I don't think I was acting strangely at this moment. I was just doing what I was born to do, what I spent my whole life training for.

He gasped. "I said stop!"

"Well, then answer my damn question!"

"I don't know names- the names specifically of people- people who buy from us -"

Slowly I crept the cables closer to the wire.

"Wait! Wait! I know the companies- the companies' names! Those are the main people who buy from us. It's not- it's not a specific person that buys, but companies."

"Names!" My voice dropped. Steady. Sharp.

"There's- there's Globeworks."

A well-known company that claimed to study the history and genetics of supernaturals, they took it too far as they dissected them as if they were exotic creatures. If they hadn't been so cruel with their research, they would've been a very helpful company and probably would've been supported by the supernatural government for trying to expand research on them.

"Midnight- Midnight Entertainment.-"

It was obvious what this company was about. Selling supernaturals into sexual slavery because there are disturbing people out there who want to own supernaturals and have complete control over their bodies.

"Blackwell Corporation!"

The cables are back on. He began struggling against his restraints and trying to dislodge the razors from inside his calf. Obviously, he was not being successful and was just burning his skin and muscle more. Though I would admit, his agony was starting to get to me. A gnawing feeling crept into my stomach as burning skin disturbed my senses.

"That place has been shut down for years," I growled.

"I'm sorry! It's just a place my father talked about! I didn't know!"

"So you've been lying to me?"

"No!"

"That's the only one I wasn't too sure of. I swear!"

I gave him a long stare, watching him pant through clenched teeth. His eyes were wild.

"Fine. Keep going!"

"Normalis Corporation!"

No shocker there! It was practically a branch of their government. Corrupt, violent, and filled with hypocrites in suits pretending they had morals.

"The People's Federation."

Oh! Shit! Everything stopped. My hand froze just inches from the cables. A chill settled over me like ice slipping down my spine.

"What did you say?"

It was almost comical how quickly he flinched. I liked the fear I instilled in him, it made this interrogation run so smoothly.

"The People's Federation," he finally muttered.

The bastards who started it all — who built the facilities, who created the assassins like me, like my siblings. They were the ones who played god with synthetic DNA, fabricating enhanced individuals like weapons on an assembly line. They weren't just some dark rumor. They were the reason I existed. But Waverly… she destroyed everything. Every lab. Every off-grid facility. Burned to the ground.

So how the hell were they back?

"How many supernaturals do they end up buying?"

"I don't know. I genuinely don't know," his voice cracked as he tried to defend himself and his hands still trembling from the last surge of pain.

"I know my business partners and the financials of the company, but not how many monsters we actually do sell."

There it was again. When will he learn to stop using that word — monsters? It was honestly his own fault for using such a disrespectful word to describe those people – those victims. He deserved the few-second shock I gave him, but it was enough to make him jolt. He really did deserve it!

"Do you know what kind of supernaturals these companies request?"

"Not typically, but- but I know Midnight Entertainment makes requests. They request that vampires get defanged."

Of course, they did. A company infamous for selling supernatural sex slaves would want the most seductive and dangerous of them all — vampires. But asking to defang them? That was next-level cruelty. Their venom wasn't just some party trick; it helped break down blood, like a leech's saliva. Without it, they'd starve.

"What about the People's Federation?" My voice came out low, measured — too calm for the storm building in my chest.

"It depends," Damien said, hesitating. "From my knowledge and what I'm guessing is that they go through cycles of wanting a specific type for a month, only to change the next."

Cyclical demand for living beings. Like they were produced. "How many do they normally want?"

He stiffened. "I told you I didn't know. We send them out in bulks."

"Explain." My tone sharpened like the edge of a blade. I was done being patient.

"I can't."

"Why?"

He looked away, jaw tightening. "Because I'm already saying too much."

My hand twitched toward the cables. "Start talking."

"I can't!"

I inched closer, my shadow swallowing his trembling form. "Start talking, or else I start ripping off your fingernails as slowly as I possibly can."

My voice was colder than it had ever been, and his breath hitched. He shook his head, eyes wide. "I can't!"

I should've felt bad reattaching the cables but I was getting frustrated. He gave me so much information. So much to incriminate himself, yet now he was withholding. Why now? What was so different about this question compared to the others? He just had to explain himself.

I ended up doing what I threatened to do. His perfectly manicured nails were soon discarded on the floor. Soon I had to detach the cables from the wire to avoid permanent and irreversible damage to his leg function. His cries echoed around the room. Echoed in my skull.

This assignment would probably stay with me for a good number of years. And I probably end up regretting it sooner or later. Regret being so monstrous and out of control. Because that's what I was — out of control, letting my anger guide my actions.

"Want to talk, or should I start ripping off limbs?"

My tone was casual—too casual for the kind of threat it carried. I could see the fear in his eyes before it spilled over.

He whimpered. He actually fucking whimpered!

"We- we send them in- in bulk," voice cracked like splintered glass. "When they reach Normalis, we have a - have a building there that organizes them to go to the company that bought them."

I stared at him, jaw clenched. Why was this so hard to tell me?

"In this building," he continued, trembling like a leaf, "the building they do modifications."

"What kind?"

The demand came sharp and immediate.

"Please, I can't say!" His voice pitched upward, verging on hysteria.

"You have to!" I stepped closer, my shadow swallowing what little light reached his sweat-slicked face.

He flinched. "We modify- modify them based on the company's request. Like the defanged vampires. But we also- we also-"

"You do what?" I could feel the dread rising, acidic in my throat.

He looked away as if the words themselves would kill him. His next breath came ragged. "Our team over there- over in Normalis. They have strict orders. Orders from my father."

"What orders?"

"You have to know it's my father! It's all my father!" His voice cracked, desperation thick in the air. He was genuinely crying. Damn!

"What orders?" I wasn't going to ask again. His eyes squeezed shut like a kid bracing for a blow.

"The team- the team is forced to sterilize them. All of them." The room went silent. A vacuum of noise after the words landed. Sterilize them?

Even the children?

"What the fuck!"

"I'm sorry! It's my father! It's all my father!"

For someone who is willing to be tortured before giving up the smallest of information, in this moment, he was quick to turn on his father. Oh, how quickly one's mind can change when one realizes the danger they are in.

"Why?"

I knew why, but I had to hear him say it.

"Please!"

"Why!?"

He flinched, then finally cracked. "So that there is less monst- supernaturals around. So that we can control their reproduction and slowly eliminate their kind!"

At that moment, I didn't care anymore.

I didn't care if he lost all mobility in his legs! I didn't care if he died of the blood loss or even electrocution!

I didn't care about him!

I didn't care, just like he didn't care about all the lives he took! All the choices that he made for those people!

I wanted him to suffer! I wanted him to suffer just like the people he hurt!

He deserved this! His family deserved this!

And yet even though I said I didn't care, I still detached the cables before I could cross that line again. He wasn't allowed to die just yet.

He wasn't allowed to die that way.

I wouldn't allow him to die so easily.

He deserved worse!

He deserved to suffer like all those people.

He deserved-

Wait.

What was that noise? Despite the agony I just put Damien through, he still cackled sadistically, "I told you I was going to fuck you up when I got out. Now here's my time! You're so screwed!"

What?

The noise. It was getting louder.

Oh fuck!

"My father isn't as stupid as you. There was no way he'd let me be exchanged for your pathetic sister! He had a plan all along. You're screwed!" I froze.

What were they going to do? Blow up the room? How was that logical?

Or maybe they were going to blow up the door and come in guns blazing? That'd be cool. It'd be something out of an action movie. Yet as much as I wanted to see that, I didn't want to fight people. So I did the next best thing.

Turning one of the tables that held my tools on its side, I kicked it as hard as I could, sending it towards the door. It impaled the metal door and from the sounds of it, a man on the other side. That would buy me a second to get a little bit of coverage before they broke down the metal door. Chances are whatever they were about to blow the door up with would have a lot of metal shrapnel and the wood from the table flying across the room. I didn't need to get hit with either.

"Run and hide like the coward you are!" Damien called out gleefully despite the blood pouring from his mouth.

Ignore him, Sean.

"Always one to run from a fight! That's what you said!"

I don't run from fights. I avoid them because I know I'll win. It doesn't matter if I pull my punches or try to let the other guy win, one way or another, my emotions get the best of me, and my opponent ends up all bloody.

"Hide! Once I'm out, I'll find you!"

"I'm going to kill you!"

"Everything you did here will come back and bite your ass!" He shouted through the chaos, voice hoarse and venom laced. I could hear desperation behind every threat. He was trying to get in my head. Trying to make me slip.

The thing about this place that I had taken Damien was its incredible network. I think it was some old train station or subway or whatever with tunnels that lead all over New Jersey. Maybe some crime organization created it to smuggle things in and out of the state? That would be something. Either way, I chose the location based on how easily one can get lost in the tunnels.

My training taught me to always have an escape plan, especially when dealing with powerful companies. Employees are never fond of assassins taking out their bosses. I found that out too many times.

But before you think I would run, the tunnels were my back up plan. I've already injured one man from the table, how many more would Mr. Crane really send to get his son? I estimated about maybe five men on the other side of the door, and if there were more, I'd deal with them or retreat into the tunnel. I had been navigating them ever since I moved to New Jersey. I originally thought they were a myth, so I had to see for myself if the tunnels were true. Lo and behold, I found them and now have a general idea of how to get through them.

But I wasn't gonna cower in them. Not like Damien fucking Crane suggested.

I was going to fight and attempt to not kill anyone. But I make no promises that I won't end up with some blood on my hands by the end of this.

Everything I was about to do would be in self-defense. That I could promise you.

Just as I expected, metal shrapnel and wood exploded into the room, but I couldn't tell from where I took cover if it had hit anything. I also had a sneaky suspicion that these men had never properly breached a hostile situation before, as soon as the explosion went off, they began shuffling in. That or they believed their explosion had killed me in an instant. In both cases, they're really stupid. I used their stupidity to my advantage. It was almost surprising how quickly I took the men out. I didn't register most of it. It's as if all my training came back to me in that instant, and I was back out in the field. Only this time, I wasn't being paid, and I wasn't trying to kill anyone. I mean, sure, a few stray bullets were flying around the room, but I shielded myself from those with the bodies of the men closest to me. Technically, I wasn't the one who killed them, just the one who initiated the threat, which these men figured they had to kill.

I'll be honest I was expecting more of a fight. These were the men that Mr. Crane assigned to retrieve his son, and yet it took me maybe five minutes to incapacitate or kill them.

Pathetic!

Utterly pathetic!

Not to mention pointless. Why did they risk their lives just to end up either seriously injured or dead? Why didn't they put up more of a fight? Why were they so stupid?

Seriously! They were so dumb!

I figured I'd be at least busy for ten to fifteen minutes. But no, these guys were definitely not trained properly. Then again, not everyone is trained to be a professional killer. Some people aren't even trained to do simple kills from a long distance. You'd think that someone like Crane, a powerful man, would invest in some professional killers to protect himself and his family. It's not like professional killers were difficult to hire. For God's sake, Waverly had her own company based on that. So why not just hire some and not these idiots?

They couldn't even protect Damien.

Oh shit.

Damien.

Oh god.

How could I have forgotten he was still tied to the chair? The chair was directly in front of the door.

Fuck!

I should've moved the chair!

Wood. Metal. Maybe even a few stray bullets. They were all lodged into the front of his body.

It was horrifying to look at.

His face and chest took the brute hit. Chunks of wood and shrapnel stuck out from his skin. I'm not sure if he still had his left eye, as a piece of metal embedded itself in the socket. Had I not known who he was, he'd be unrecognizable with how quickly his face swelled up — how disturbing he looked.

I should've moved him away from the door.

This was on me. His blood was on me.

"You-" he rasped, his voice nearly drowned in gurgling breath, "You didn't run."

Despite how grotesque he looked, he still managed to let out a strained chuckle. From all I've seen, this might've been one of the most disturbing things I've seen in my career. I don't know how he was still alive at this moment, let alone laughing.

"No," I said softly, "I didn't run."

"I- I should have. I should have picked you." His voice cracked, barely audible.

"You should have, but I would have caused you more trouble."

He tried to laugh, only to cough instead, and blood came up, too. The signs of death were creeping up.

"Can I- can I have that thing?"

"That thing- the thing you gave me-"

I already knew what he wanted. I wasn't entirely cruel.

Obviously, I pierced the nanobyte back into his skin.

Despite all I've said, nobody deserves to die in immense agony.

"Thank- thank you." His voice barely hung on.

⁓⁓

I stayed with him until he took his last staggered breath. It's the least I could do. He didn't deserve to go out that way. Plus, I had to confirm the kill – something I always had to do. Something that was embedded in my mind to do.

I wanted to feel guilty for putting him in this situation, only to remember the amount of lives he had done the same to. I guess I can only really say to him in this moment – even if he was no longer alive – was RIP Damien fucking Crane.

Then I reached down and took back the nanobyte.

No use wasting a good tool.

FAMILY BONDS

They say you never forget your first dead body. I'm not entirely sure who actually said it, but I know someone said it. They say it because it had something to do with the emotions you felt at that moment and how you initially reacted. However, it was after that that you become almost numb to seeing them, no matter how many times you find yourself staring death in the face.

I really wish I knew who said it. Then I could go punch them in the face for being so stupid. It was apparent that whoever said it had never taken a life before – obviously they were just talking about losing your loved one and seeing their lifeless body afterward.

When you're the reason that somebody's dead, you never forget it, no matter if it's your first dead body or your seventieth. That person's life ended at your hands. You had their blood on your hands. And no matter how much you wash your hands, it'll always be there — even if you can't see it. That blood was a stain on your soul and mind, forever there.

I really hate that Damien fucking Crane was now on my list of dead bodies I could never forget.

I fucking hated it!

But his blood was on my hands. I should've moved him.

I hated it! I hated feeling this way!

It wasn't fair!

Why did I have to be born into the world like this? Why?!

I should've had a normal birth, a normal childhood, been a normal teenager, and had a normal early adulthood. Instead,

I had this. The stupid ability that made me different — forced me to be a killer.

It wasn't fair!

I just wanted a normal life. One where I didn't have blood on my hands since I was the age of five. It wasn't fucking fair!

I shouldn't have these traumatic memories, memories of taking lives just because someone paid me. I shouldn't have blood on my hands. Staining my soul.

I shouldn't have Damien Crane's blood on my hands.

But I did. I never got the normal childhood I wanted, and I killed people for money. That's the kind of person I was.

That's the kind of person I was created to be. And that's the kind of person I had to be to get Pearl back.

I had to be a killer.

Not just any killer, but the assassin who was trained day and night to be the best of the best.

So I guess Mr. Crane better look the fuck out because I was coming for him. And this time, I was purposely trying to get his blood on my hands.

He fucked with the wrong family.

I was going to protect Pearl.

I would always protect Pearl!

"Again!"

"Again!"

"Again!"
"You should only be punching once!"

"Again!"

"One punch. One deadly punch."

"Again!"

"Are you stupid?"
"Punch again!"
"Quite a stupid boy, aren't you, SS1051?"

"Again!"
"Stupid! Punch harder!"
"Stupid boy! Again!"
It never mattered how bloody my fists got. I had to keep punching until I got it right.
"Again!"

"Again!"
"Enough! You are stupid. You are not getting this."
"A failure is what you are!"
"A pathetic puncher."
"You're pathetic."
"At least we have more like you that can get it right."
"Bring in the sister. Maybe she'll be better."
My fist shot through his gut, shattering every bone in its path. As he toppled over, I didn't stop my assault, making his face the prime target for my punches. I didn't stop. I couldn't stop. He had to be unrecognizable. He had to be broke, just like he was trying to do to me.
"No one touches her!"

"SS1051!"
"Hands up!"
"On the ground!"

"Hands behind your back!"

"Get the body out of here!"

The normal protocol if anyone killed a trainer — wasn't my first time.

"SS1051 stand!"

"Give us the soiled clothes."

"Change!"

Another protocol, get rid of the evidence so we weren't sticky when we went back to training. They didn't want to deter our practice.

"SS1051, explain what happened!"

"Why did you kill another one?"

"I thought-"

"Speak up!"

"I thought he told me to punch again!"

"So you punched him?"

"it was an accident."

"Speak up!"

"It was an accident! I was facing him when he said again!"

"SS1051, one more incident, and you know what happens!"

Termination.

Nobody ever sees the children who get sent to termination.

I can't be sent there.

Who'd protect her?

"SS1051, do you understand?"

"I understand!"

"Good, now go again!"

The other side of the room could be seen through the small fist-sized hole.

"Good!"

"Keep going!"

"Again!"

"Sir?"

"Maybe we won't need the other one if this one proves to be our successor."

"What will we do to the other?"

"We'll have to see how SS1051 does, but if it proves to be successful, then we send the other to termination."

"Keep monitoring it. See if it improves with the following instructions properly and can keep up with the deadly punch."

They'd terminate her if I kept being successful.

I couldn't be successful, but I couldn't be the worst either. I have to protect her. But how can I do that without sending her or myself to termination? What was the median of being both horrible and a success? How could I do that without them catching on?

<hr>

I wasn't entirely sure what day they came or at what time, all I know is I was supposed to be on the sleeping shift when I heard the commotion. I didn't know who was outside attacking the facility members, but I didn't care. Whoever they were, they earned my respect. However, it didn't stop me from running out into the hallway to find my sister. All my adrenaline and fighting instinct had one purpose, finding and protecting her. I never stopped running even though around me the facility members were dropping like flies. I think one of them tried to grab me, but as soon as I felt his fingers pry on my arm, I bent their fingers back, dislocating them with ease. I only had one purpose and nothing was going to stop that.

I can't remember where I had found her whether it was in the mess hall or one of the training rooms, but I found her. She was small then — so small that I could easily wrap my body around her and take the brute hit of any danger that was coming. That's what I did. I covered my entire body over hers, and she tucked herself into my chest. Nobody was going to hurt her. And I whispered, over and over:

"Shhhhh."

"I'm here. I'll protect you."

"You're going to be okay."

"I'm here."

It wasn't long after I had found her that they ended up finding us. At first, I thought I was hallucinating, that somehow I was no longer on this plane of existence. The woman who came over to us looked ethereal, how was I supposed to know if she was real or not? And yet, she came down to our level and offered me her hand, not saying anything. There is something in her eyes, though, something like a promise. A promise of safety and comfort. It was something I had never seen in a person's eyes before, especially in eyes that looked like amethysts.

I don't know if it was a good thing that I unwrapped myself from my sister and took the stranger's hand, but I did it. The stranger offered her other hand to my sister, but she never took it. She was a lot smarter than me in that sense — never trusting a stranger who said nothing to us. Instead, she clung to the back of my shirt, and soon, I tucked her under my arm as we made our way out of the facility.

I think that was the first time she had ever seen the sky, up close. We weren't allowed outside the facility doors until we reached a certain age. I think it was six or seven — that's around the age they expected us to be able to survive alone. My sister wasn't that age yet. She had never seen the outside. Never been past the facility doors. She was only able to look at the sky – see the sun, moon, and stars – from the television or the skyline that was in the mess hall.

I was happy to have been there with her when she first experienced it. To see her face light up, breathing in the fresh air and feeling grass for the first time. It's something I never wanted to forget. But it also made me realize how much more I wanted her to experience and be there when she did. I wanted to see the excitement, the wonder in her eyes when she encountered something new. That's something I got to see right away as the strangers took us and several other children to an aircraft parked a few kilometers away from the facility.

I swear, we all had the same expression upon seeing the massive object. None of us had ever seen something so great, so new. It was amazing to see what the machine could do, how it functioned and was able to carry us miles into the air — miles away from the facility. It was truly an amazing experience. And watching it land was also one of the most intriguing and wonderful experiences that any of us could've had. I couldn't imagine what it would be like to have power over such a great machine, to be able to operate it properly. It was something I wish I could've done. It would've been so exciting and freeing to be able to do what the pilot did. In another life, that's what I would have been.

You know, it's at moments that I remember how naive we were. Here, we were following complete strangers, and they were leading us to a building that looked eerily similar to the facility — only this building was bigger. It looked homier than the facility did. We were naive not to question where they were taking us and what they wanted with us. We just blindly followed the strangers as they welcomed us to what they called our "safe haven" — a place where we'd be treated properly and provided the comfort we deserved.

Obviously, that comfort didn't last as long as they hoped. But either way, they gave us a new sense of ourselves and allowed us to believe we were more than just killing machines.

It was only when we settled that the strangers finally introduced themselves, the ethereal one being Waverly — even her name sounded celestial. The other was Katya, who didn't really interact with us but rather tended to stay by Waverly's side and observe us. Katya remained a stranger to most of us until we were much older — she waited until we were mature enough to understand her own trauma and experiences. I think we reminded her of herself and her childhood with all the torment she had to overcome.

Either way, Waverly was kind and warm towards us, giving us anything we desired to be comfortable. Even help us settle into a space to make it our own, something we were never allowed to do at the facility.

When it came time to introduce ourselves to her and the people who worked with her, most of us were left unsure. We didn't have names, but we did have acronyms and numbers, so that's what we told her.

"TP0065"

"SS1000."

"H0091"

"SS1051."

"PK0305."

"SS1201."

"MM0219."

It was only after we all finished giving our codes that she realized that's how we were addressed. We weren't treated like people. We weren't treated like children. We were just machines, so why did we deserve a name?

I think it was right after we were fully settled in our rooms that she had us all join her in what seemed like a giant office decorated with paper all over the walls. Each paper contained lines upon lines of names. She wanted us to choose whichever stuck out to us, and that's who we would be from now on. It felt empowering to be able to choose who we wanted to be — it gave us the right amount of control back in our lives. And so, one by one, we all begin choosing names for ourselves, even though it was difficult to choose just one and stick with it. The amount of times we'd say one name and then a few hours later, we'd want another one.

Eventually, some of us chose names that stuck, and Waverly created birth certificates and adoption papers with our chosen names on them. She was giving us a life – an opportunity to be someone. Meanwhile, others, like myself, struggled to come up with a name. It was difficult choosing who I wanted to be and what name really resonated with me. My little sister, too, felt the same.

Who are we to become? What name defined who we really were?

It was a rather difficult choice, one that shouldn't have been taken lightly. And yet my older half-sister, the one who shared the same genetic ability as me and my younger sister, easily chose the name Tilly — Teresa Ila Lily Lola Yasmin. She wanted all the names that she figured best represented her and combined them into Tilly. I'll be honest, I don't think any of those names truly represented her. She didn't reflect a semblance of warmth like the name Teresa suggested or the purity and innocence of a lily. She was a killer like any of us. Tilly had killed probably more trainers than me, and yet she still went with the name Tilly to represent the nature that she believed she had.

For my own name, it took me weeks and weeks to even remotely find something I liked, and even then, it didn't match who I wanted to be. It wasn't until this old — not that he looked at — man came over to me, introduced himself as Spencer Barnes, Waverly's father, and asked me who I was. I felt ashamed. I couldn't give him a name, it was embarrassing. Yet he smiled at me, offering to help. He offered numerous name suggestions, but Sean was the one that stuck in my brain.

Spencer explained how he knew a young man back when he was younger and a soldier during the Cold War — whatever that was. He had met a guy even younger than himself, Sean Philip Johnson who Spencer claimed had a fighting spirit much like my own. However, unlike Spencer, Sean Philip Johnson never survived the genetic altering experiment. He had died not long after the injection was introduced into his system, but Spencer never forgot him, no matter how long ago it was. Spencer suggested the name as a way of showing how names could live on for years — generations — and still have some meaning behind them. Sean Philip Johnson was someone Spencer respected dearly and wanted someone close to him to share the name. How I felt after he had told me that story was hard to explain, I had never felt something like that before. My eyes pricked with tears, but I wasn't sad. I had never cried like that before.

When I finally finished crying, Spencer told me to not feel pressured into choosing a name. Even though names were how people identified themselves and who they were, I shouldn't feel like I had to choose a name that was powerful and unique. Spencer said that no matter what name I chose, it was always going to reflect me, reflect the soft-hearted boy he had met that day.

In the end, I chose the name Sean. I wanted to be remembered for all my successes and good nature rather than the people I killed. I didn't want to be tied down to the machine I was made to be. I wanted to be a person — someone who flew those giant machines and was able to feel free.

Oh how that desire of mine was quickly washed away once the program started.

As for my younger sister, she pressured me to come up with her name, as all the ones she suggested were childish, like Giggles or Bubbles — though both represented her personality well.

As hard as I found it to choose my own name, choosing hers was ten times more difficult. It was hard to find the perfect name that best represented her and all she was — this bright, innocent, peppy little girl who found happiness in the smallest of things. What name would best fit her? Who would she become with this name?

Once again, Spencer, who insisted I begin calling him Grandpa Spencer, came by to visit and to check up on us children. I don't remember the day, but he found me and my little sister hanging around outside as she picked flowers. I remembered him asking me whether or not we had come up with a name for her. I once again felt ashamed. It was on me to pick her name, and I had failed to do so. She was expecting me to.

Grandpa Spencer offered no suggestions this time and instead said that no matter the name I chose, she would always be my precious little pearl. Even though we had been through all those adversities and struggles, she came out shining and full of innocence. My sister beamed at the nickname he gave her, and soon everyone, including myself, began calling her Pearl. She was my precious little Pearl — my precious little sister. That's who she would always be, who she was meant to be. That's who she was.

So much for Grandpa Spencer not suggesting any names.

The program started shortly after we had just become situated with our new lives.

It followed after more children — children like me, who came from facilities like mine — began being rescued by Waverly and her team. Waverly took down dozens of facilities, taking every child with her to give them a better life. Only for the government to laugh in her face and make a program that would ruin their lives. All because the government thought there were too many of us, which might have been true, but we never noticed. Waverly took great care of us and helped many of us find loving, supportive families to raise us — even if half the people who adopted us were her own family. Either way, she gave us everything, and the government ripped it away.

They didn't care about who we were, our names, or who we were to others. They only cared about what made us different – what we were originally made to do. The government made the program to control who we were just because we weren't born under proper circumstances. To make matters worse, they also forced Waverly's own children into the program as if they were just like us. As if they were born to be machines too.

The government hated what we were, and what we could do and wanted to take advantage of it — take advantage of all our previous training and make a profit. They used us to get rid of competitors and threats to their safety. Then, they opened the program up to the wealthy for them to do the same.

The government sacrificed our childhood, our comfort — and our lives — just for control and power. And had it not been for Waverly and her lawyer, the government would have taken our money too. Every life they made us take, every person we were forced to hurt, would have been for nothing. Our trauma would have been for nothing had Waverly not stepped in and made a clause that gave us some profit. Later, she would go on to make another clause that would stop us from being sued for taking someone's life on the accord of someone hiring us. We weren't the ones at fault, we were just the ones who were forced to do the actions — the actions of someone else.

In the end, the government got what it wanted with the program, many of us were at their beck and call, ready to make a decent buck for whatever job they had for us. Most of us even ended up turning on each other, which made sense as we were all fighting to have some sort of control in our lives — control being in the form of money. The program took many of our lives. The government wanted less of us, and that's what they got. So many ended their lives as the amount of blood on our hands and bodies at our feet became too much. It was too difficult for us to continue, especially with our mental health deteriorating.

The government got what it wanted, destroying the childhood of many of us and making us into monsters — the machines we were originally made to be. They were cruel.

None of us ever deserved this.

My precious little Pearl didn't deserve the blood that was forced on her hands.

Life inside of the program is just how you'd expect. You wake up one morning and were told about an assignment that you were chosen to complete. They give you a rundown of who your assignment was, what they did for a living, and their schedule if we had it, if not, then we have to monitor them for a few days to pick up their routine. Then, whether they were chosen to be tortured or killed, we would go and complete our assignment – though most often, people who hired us would choose to have us kill our assignments. It was always a shock to have a tortured assignment rather than a killed one — something that happened once every two months, maybe. As soon as all the information was given to you, you'd be whisked away to wherever the target was, and you'd have to monitor them for at least a day, if not more, to figure out the perfect method to kill them. If it was an easy kill, great, I could be back home within 24 hours at the mission. If the person who hired us wanted information, chances are I'd be gone for a few days. That's how life in the program went.

On days we had off when we weren't chosen for an assignment, Waverly made us study. But it was not torture methods or ways of being better at our jobs. No, she wanted

142

us to be well-educated. Waverly hired tutors and professors from local universities to teach us, paying them handsomely so we could receive a well-rounded education. I think she was the only one who had hope that the program would one day be shut down, and that when it did, we'd be able to go to an actual school, to learn like normal kids. It was wishful thinking on her part, and the program went on for many more years. Either way, she tried so hard to provide us with comfort and a sense of normalcy when we were far beyond that. I wish I had thanked her for how hard she tried to give us a snippet of a normal life.

When it came to Pearl, I never let her take long assignments, the ones where she'd be gone for days. Waverly and I had some kind of unspoken deal that none of those assignments would be given to her. Plus, if she was given an assignment, and I wasn't too busy, I was there with her, giving her as much guidance as I could and desperately trying to preserve her innocence. Tilly would always laugh when we returned, saying how Pearl didn't need her big brother watching her every move, calling me pathetic for hovering. I didn't care what Tilly thought. I would do everything in my power to keep Pearl from seeing the true darkness of our jobs, even if that meant me tagging along and completing the assignments for her.

If I'm being honest, it began to take a toll on my mental health. Many times I had seen other assassins like myself fall into this depressive state. Many times, we'd find their bodies somewhere around the compound because the work became too much. It terrified me when I became more irritable, stopped eating at points, and even stopped coming out of my room. I just wanted to be left alone. I didn't want to face anyone. Didn't want them to see me broken and weak. I felt like every day, I would just struggle to even pull myself out of bed. I had stopped taking jobs during this time. I just didn't want to leave my room. Who could blame me, really? I distance myself from Waverly, Grandpa Spencer, Pearl, and everyone. I couldn't face them.

And yet, one day, it all changed. I found solace in something that I always ignored.

A girl.

She was a part of Waverly's family — I think the second cousin of Waverly on her mother's side. Her name was Ayla, and everything about her was perfect. She was around a similar age to me, though I think I might've been a few months older if anything, but she was everything. Sure, I had seen her when I was first brought to the compound, but back then, I was a child. I wasn't thinking about girls or anything like that. Now, it was different, she was beautiful and somehow brought sparkling light into my dark life. I can't remember why she came to visit on this particular day, but I just remember coming out of my room for the first time in weeks and wanting to be near her. There was something about her that made her unique from others. She was human, and yet — the moment she touched an instrument, it was like the world around you faded. Her music could shift the air in the room, pull you out of whatever hell you were in, and wrap you in whatever emotion she felt. If she was joyful, you smiled. If she was grieving, your heart ached. She didn't just play — she transported you. I loved sitting in the lounge and listening to her play. Watching her get lost in the rhythm. It made me forget all the shittiness that was in my life — all the sadness and anger I was bottling inside. All of it was just gone as soon as I heard her and saw her. When she started visiting more frequently, I opened myself up again. I no longer avoided the family and instead spent my free time doing things with them. Ayla brought life back into me.

"Sean's got a crush!"

"Shut it, pipsqueak," I hissed, glancing over my shoulder. "she might hear."

"Wats da prableuh whif thaf?"

Pearl's words came out muffled. I shouldn't have put my hand over her mouth. It would probably raise more suspicions, especially with her mumbling behind my hand.

"What did you say, P?"

She folded her arms across her tiny chest like she was ten feet tall.

"I said, what's the problem with that?" I rubbed the back of my neck, suddenly feeling very exposed.

"Firstly, I don't have a crush on her," I said, not very convincingly. "And secondly, I don't think she wants any association with me outside of this."

Pearl tilted her head, confused but determined. "You're nice and strong. Why wouldn't she like you?"

"It's more complicated than that, P," I said gently, crouching to her level. "You have to be older to understand."

"I'm old enough," she said proudly. "I'm seven. I'm smart."

I smiled. "I know you are, but this is more complex than just liking one another."

Before she could argue back, a new voice chimed in, light and teasing from just behind me. "Who's liking who?"

I could've had a heart attack right then. I thought it was Ayla, but thankfully, it was just Bexley and Curtis. Curtis was Waverly's son – her biological son – and the one who spent the most time with us – the adopted children. As for Bexley and Curtis, those two were as thick as thieves, always being where the other was. I'm also pretty sure they slept in the same room together. But their relationship was anything but romantic, I think they just found comfort in each other. Plus, from what I've heard, over eavesdropping on some conversations, Curtis's mind was peaceful and quiet, and it gave Bex a way of escaping her ability. I don't know how his mind could be so calm and quiet. He had also been through a lot of shit, much like the rest of us. Yet somehow, it never weighed on him — it made me sort of jealous.

"Nobody likes-"

"Sean likes Ayla!"

"Seriously, P! Be quiet!"

Of course, right as I went to grab her, she scurried behind Curtis, knowing damn well I would never purposely try to fight with him to get her. She was such a little punk.

"Hey, what's so wrong with you liking her? Ayla probably feels honored."

Bexley leaned against the doorway, smirking. "Oh yeah, a tough guy like you is exactly what she wants."

I don't know if either of them was being sarcastic, but it sure sounded like it. They know exactly why it was wrong for her to know I liked her — not that I did! She just brought me comfort in my time of need. Almost like she knew exactly what song to play to help me calm my emotions. But it wasn't like I had romantic feelings for her. I couldn't have feelings for her.

Pearl, of course, wasn't done. "Sean and Ayla sitting in a tree k-i-s-s-i-n-g—"

I spun around. "Where the hell did you learn that song?"

"What even is it?" Curtis asked, confused.

"Grandpa told me," Pearl said proudly. "All about this song, it's for when people like like each other."

I scoffed. "Well, I think the feeling needs to be mutual, and Ayla doesn't like me."

Oh shit.

Wait a second!

"I didn't mean it like that!"

"Ohhh, but you said it," Bex sang with a wicked grin.

"Sean has a crush on Ayla!" Pearl squealed.

"Pearl! Shut up!"

Curtis held up both hands. "Leave her alone, Sean. She's just excited for her big brother."

"Just stop! All of you!" My voice cracked louder than I wanted. The teasing stung more than it should've. I couldn't deal with their teasing. It was bad enough I was getting it from a seven-year-old. I didn't need those two to start, too. Plus, they didn't get it. Nobody did.

"Maybe we should cut him loose with the teasing?" Bex murmured, her tone finally softening.

"But why Bex?" Pearl asked, frowning at her.

"Just because he doesn't need to be teased for something he can't control."

I never heard the rest of the conversation as I had already wandered too far out of the hearing range. But whatever else was said made the teasing stop, and I never heard about it again. I was thankful for Bexley stepping in and stopping Pearl from telling the whole world. She was more of an older sister to me and Pearl than our own sister. Bex cared more about our mental and physical health, meanwhile, Tilly asked about how our kills were and if we did it properly. I guess that's the outcome of some people's personalities who are in the facility longer than others, they don't care about your emotional state, just if you did the job right. I don't blame her, though she was born before any of us. All of the people in the batch she was made either were killed as infants or faced termination. Tilly didn't have anyone who was her age or knew the struggles that she endured. I think that's why she moved away as soon as she turned eighteen — she didn't have the same support as any of us. Tilly's been gone for a few years now. None of us have really heard from her, but Waverly assured us she was still alive. And if Waverly said it, we believed it. Though now that I thought about it, I doubted Waverly would've told us if Tilly was dead, Pearl was still learning the concept of familial loss and how to mourn. Pearl was still young — still too innocent for this world.

"You know, I think that one guy has a thing for you."
"Which guy?"
I shouldn't have been listening in, yet as soon as I heard her melodic voice, I just had to stop and listen. It was almost as if she enchanted me with her voice.
"I don't know names! That one guy who always hangs around when we're in the lounge."
"Oh, because that's so specific, Marcus," she replied with a light laugh.
That lucky guy she always brought when she came to visit. I knew they were just friends —probably best friends — but it still made my stomach twist when I saw them whispering and laughing with each other. It was unfair that he got to be so close to her all the time and got to listen to her play any instrument whenever he asked. It wasn't fair! I wanted that. I needed to hear her play more than him! I deserved to be there to watch her successes.
But I swear I didn't have any romantic feelings for her.

I was just jealous of his privilege.

"He's the awkward one. He throws baseballs and tennis balls at the wall when you stop playing."

Screw him! I was trying to fill the silence as she took breaks and was practicing my hand-eye coordination.

"Oh, Sean!" she said with a little laugh.

Her just saying my name sent shivers up my spine. She said it so sweetly.

"That's the guy. He definitely has a thing for you."

I did not!

"I don't think he does, Marcus."

Thank you! Wait-

Why would she say it in that tone? Why did it sound like she would be glad if I didn't?

"C'mon, Ayla, the guy barely hangs around the lounge unless you're there. He's totally in love with you."

I'm not in love with her! I just like her music.

"You have been here wayyyyy too many times. It's very stalkerish of you to know where he hangs out."

"Shut up."

I can just imagine them bumping shoulders and chuckling to themselves. It made me sick to think about that.

"I'm just saying he's not the worst person to have liked you."

"Marcus, stop already. I told you I wasn't feeling any sort of relationship with anyone. You need to stop pushing that on me."

"I'm sorry, I'm just worried you're going to be all alone when you move here. I don't want you to not have anyone."

She was moving here! Why didn't I know that before? Was I going to see her more with that guy? Was she going to visit more? Why was she moving up here?

It wasn't like her dad lived around here. I think the last time Waverly talked to him, he was somewhere in Mexico or was it Jamaica? Either way, he was nowhere around here, so why would Ayla move up here? To be closer to the family?

I wanted to know why. Yet I never did find out.

I was sent on an assignment that lasted a week, and I never got to talk to her about it. She also stopped visiting soon after, which made no sense to me.

She had moved to New York for a reason and was closer to her family. Yet she never visited them, not anymore. It was almost like she disappeared off the face of the world, and yet, her musical talent still haunted me. I swear I could hear her strumming on the guitar or playing concerto or even just humming late at night. It was both horrible and soothing, as hearing it would calm me down almost instantly.

But I swear I didn't have a thing for her. I couldn't.

There was only one thing I could truly and deeply care about in my life. That was Pearl.

I couldn't waste my time on a girl who never thought twice about me. I could only focus on Pearl.

She was the one who needed all my attention.

I had to protect her.

⌒⌒

I think the program shut down a few months after my nineteenth birthday, but I could never remember the specific date — sometime in the winter. Of course, the worst part of our lives had to get shut down during the worst season. Thankfully, Pearl and I didn't stick around for the cold weather and moved to Florida with Bexley — though leaving Waverly behind after all she had done was heartbreaking. Thankfully, Waverly understood, she knew that we had to go and find ourselves in the world. Make names for ourselves that didn't tie us to the program. Bexley was quick to move on, as she was almost instantly staying in Florida and finding love. It was insanely crazy how fast she could move on with her life, as if the last eight or nine years in the program hadn't traumatized her. Or the fact that we were literally born in a lab and made to be killers. How did she do it? How could she just push past everything?

If I'm being honest, I think the guy she was seeing had something to do with it. Around him, she was like a completely different person. It was terrifying. That's what love could do to a person, change them into something the complete opposite of what they were, or so I heard. But she was a killer through and through, just like any of us, and yet with the boyfriend, she was just Bexley. The Bexley that worked as a waitress at some country club and spent time watching rom-coms and stupid movies. It was almost like the Bexley I knew, the one who made men scratch their faces off to get her out of their heads, was gone. But obviously, that wasn't true. She just did a good job burying that side of her.

I wish I could have done that.

I tried so hard to do that.

Even as I worked at the same country club as Bex, I tried to forget who I used to be and tried to live in the present. Yet, when you're dealing with drunk, wealthy assholes who demand things from you, it's hard to forget where you came from. At least I didn't hurt any of them, even though I desperately wanted to. Well, it didn't hurt them physically, I should say. There were occasions where I'd accidentally charge them the expensive type of liquor but only give them the bottom shelf kind.

What can I say? I was an asshole myself.

It's not like they didn't deserve it or have the money to afford stuff like that. They had club memberships, for god sake. Obviously, they could have afforded my scams. They deserved it, especially with how they treated staff. Specifically, how they treated the women employees. It was like they were horn dogs trying to get the simplest attention from them. And the number of times they would put their hands on the female staff was insane. They were lucky I was only scamming them for their money and not doing what my thoughts screamed for me to do. I wanted to hurt them so badly. Yet every time I wanted to lose my shit on them, Bexley would force me to take a break.

Probably so I wouldn't break them.

At least outside of work, I could have somewhat of a normal life, not that I did much. When I wasn't working, I spent my free time at Bexley's house, avoiding any social contact. Sure, I saw everyone who was staying at Bex's house and her boyfriend on occasion, but those were people I was used to. I never went out to parties or anything like that, even though I'd be invited numerously. Partying just wasn't for me.

The times I did end up leaving the house were to pick Pearl up from her elementary school, and that was always exhausting. Not because seeing my precious little sister finally getting an education was bad, but rather because it was the other students' moms and the teachers. On the days that I was there for Pearl, it seemed like all attention was focused on me. I wouldn't say I was a bad-looking guy, but I definitely didn't like how many eyes watched me. Not to mention the gossip I would overhear about me.

"Oh, he's so young." Their voices drifted just a few feet away, soft and judgmental, like a flock of birds circling something unfamiliar.

"He's such a good dad picking up his daughter."

Wrong, but thanks for the assumption.

"Do you think he's single?"

"Do you think that he and that woman have split custody?"

What woman?

"They're both so young to have a little girl her age."

"I feel bad for the little one."

Though sometimes the wording changed, it was all the same version of the questions and comments. They assumed Pearl was my child, which made no sense because she was only seven and a bit years younger than me — maybe eight years younger. Plus, I never wanted kids, nor would I ever have one with Bexley, that was all kinds of wrong in my mind. Secondly, they thought Bex and I were a couple, which would NEVER happen — she was my older sister, no doubt about that. Finally, they should've minded their own business. I was there to pick up my little sister, and that was it. There was no drama, no reason for them to ever discuss us, and yet they still did. It was frustrating.

If I'm being honest I think Waverly should've prepared us for moments like these, the gossiping women and the grabby old men. That was one thing she should've focused on when giving us a well-rounded education, helping us find ways to work around situations like these. Ways for these problems to not impact you so much.

I hated the grabby old men.

I hated the chatty women in the schoolyard.

I hated all this normalcy.

Is this truly what the world was like? Could people really not just focus on themselves and not drag other people into their messes or conversation topics?

I guess that's always how it's been. Even as an assassin, we were the conversation topics of many people, and we were always being dragged to deal with people's messes. So why was living in Florida with these situations much worse than being an assassin? Was I really programmed to choose violence and murder over telling people to stop? Was I truly a broken human? Was I even really human?

Why was I struggling so much to find normalcy in my life? Why couldn't I just suck it up for Pearl?

Why couldn't I be normal for Pearl?

I just wanted to be good enough for her, good enough to protect her properly.

"Alright, Sean. What's with the pouty face?" A voice cut through the noise of my thoughts like a pin popping a balloon.

I had just gotten home from a double shift at the country club — one bartending shift and a training shift to be a security guard. I was hoping to make some extra cash and not spend my evenings alone anymore. Sure, I would help Pearl with her homework if she needed it, but most of the time, she didn't. Plus, I was getting tired of being the third wheel whenever Bex and her boyfriend were watching movies. Picking up a new shift was the best decision I could've made, especially with how much overtime I was doing. So, to say the least, I was exhausted I couldn't properly regulate my emotions. Thus, my face showed how I was feeling.

"I'm just tired." I muttered the words while rubbing the back of my neck, hoping that would be enough to shut the conversation down.

"Uh-huh, you sure about that?"

Bex arched a brow, skeptical as always. She leaned against the counter, arms folded, her tone halfway between teasing and concerned.

"No, but I don't want to drag you into anything."

"Please, I'm not going to overreact." She scoffed before I could even respond.

"That's bullshit."

Of course, Mina decided to speak up at that moment. She was one of the other residents staying at the house, but she wasn't like us. I mean, yes, she was a part of a program somewhat like ours, but she didn't have abilities like us. She was an orphan, she wasn't created in a lab nor created to be a machine. Even though she wasn't as special as us, she was still family.

"What was that M?" Bex called from the kitchen, already winding herself up.

"I said, it's bullshit that you won't overreact. You always do."

"You gonna take that slander, Bex?" I asked with a dry chuckle, hoping to lighten the mood.

"Stay out of this, Sean! What did I overreact about?"

"What don't you overreact about?"

"Why were you out so late?"

"Who were you with?"

"Is that a boy?" You always have to be up in my business and overreact when I tell you stuff." Mina pitched her voice high. I wish I could say her mockery of Bexley's voice was uncanny, but I couldn't lie.

"I'm up in your business because you disappear days at a time, and I'm worried about your well-being! And I don't overreact!"

"You're overreacting right now!"

"Wha- Oh! Shut up! Go back to your game!"

Ah yes! A typical Wednesday night at our house. Everyone yelling and fighting, but that's how we tried to show we cared. Bex turned her attention back to me, her eyes narrowing with concern.

"Now, what's going on with you?"

I sighed and leaned heavier against the back of the couch. "The moms are talking again and now I think it's getting worse because now I always see them at the club."

"Sean, you just have to ignore them."

"That's easy for you to say," I grumbled. "You can move around the club. I'm stuck in one place with beverages that make people spill their darkest secrets to me."

"I get that," Bex said, "but you just need to brush off their comments and get a laugh out of them. I mean, come on, some of those conversations are hilarious."

"Maybe for you."

She gave me a pointed look. "I know it's not easy, but you can't go around punching and beating people up because they did or said something that bothered you. That's not how this life works."

"You're one to talk! I know what you did yesterday. That guy by the pool was becoming awfully friendly with you, and next thing — boom — he's slamming into one of the waiter's carts and falling into the pool."

"He was drunk," she said quickly.

I could have believed her had her tone not been defensive.

I narrowed my eyes. "That's interesting because I don't remember him coming up to the bar for any drinks nor seeing you come up with an order."

"Okay! Whatever!" she snapped. "What do you want me to say?!"

"Just admit you're being hypocritical."

She huffed, then crossed her arms. "Fine! I'm a hypocrite. I used my abilities to send the asshole into the pool. There! Is that what you wanted to hear?"

"Yes! I want you to admit that it's not so easy."

Bex's voice softened, frustration giving way to honesty. "Okay, it's difficult to ignore the call of my abilities, but I still attempt to not use them. You don't, Sean!"

"It's hard!" I shot back. "Not all of us have concealable abilities that don't show physical damage to a person! I did what I had to do."

"You put a guy in a hospital."

"And I'd do it again if I had a choice. He was spiking people's drinks! And it's not like I hurt the perp on company time."

"No, but if he wakes up and tells the cops your description, you're so screwed."

"Key words "if he wakes up", and if he does, chances are he doesn't remember a thing. I threw his head into the wall enough times he won't know a thing."

"That's not the point!"

"Then what is!"

Bex crossed her arms, her voice sharp with exasperation. "You need to control yourself. You're not with Mom anymore, so you can't just act all impulsively. You need to look out for yourself and Pearl."

"I am doing that!"

"No, you aren't. You're endangering yourself by getting involved in minor situations."

"Yes, because someone being drugged is a minor situation."

"That's not what I meant," she said, quieter this time but still firm. "I just mean, I don't want to see you behind bars because you got involved in something you couldn't punch your way out of."

"Whatever!" I snapped. "I'm not going to end up behind bars!"

"You don't know that!"

"Yeah, I do!"

"Ugh! You don't listen!"

"Neither do you, so just stop!"

I couldn't take her mothering crap much longer. Instead of sticking around to fight with her some more, I turned my back and went up the stairs to my room.

"Are you kidding me, Sean?" she called after me. "Come back here! I'm not done!"

"Just leave him, Bex," Mina chimed in from the living room. "You both need to cool down."

"Oh, go back to your game, Mina!"

I didn't need to cool down, I just needed to be away from Bexley. Sometimes — most times — she could be too much. It didn't help that she knew your thoughts and feelings before you could even voice them. It was so annoying and unfair! Sometimes I just wanted to hate her.

"You don't listen!" Yeah, well fuck you too!" I muttered under my breath as I shut my bedroom door a little too hard.

Why did she have to be so much today? What was her problem? Normally she was mothering and sometimes bitchy, but today it was almost like everything was off. What was her problem?

"Are you done screaming at each other?"

What the shit!

"Pearl, what are you doing in my room?"

She blinked at me, arms crossed like I was the one in trouble. "I was looking for your fancy art pens. I have a poster that I need to do for school, and I think they'd look great with the poster board."

"You could have asked me before breaking into my room and snooping."

"I wasn't snooping! I just wanted your pens."

"You could have waited until I was home and in my room before coming in here!"

Her eyes narrowed. "What crawled up your ass!?"

"Hey! Language!"

"What? You swear all the time!"

"I'm a grown-up. I can swear. You can't."

"Screw you!"

"Hey! Enough of that!" I pointed toward the door. "I've already had to deal with one bitchy sister, I'm not about to deal with another. Got that?"

She huffed. "Yeah, whatever."

"Good. Now go wait outside my room so I can change and then I'll give you the pens."

"Ok, fine!" I raised an eyebrow.

"What was that?"

She sighed, defeated. "Okay, thank you Sean, for the help."

"That's what I thought. Now out." She stomped off, mumbling under her breath, and shut the door behind her.

Seriously! What was going on today with the girls? What was with the high emotions and yelling? Was it me? Maybe Bex was right, I acted impulsively. Was it all my fault?

"Hey, Pearl," I said, my voice quieter this time. "I'm sorry, I've had an exhausting day, and I don't mean to take it out on you girls."

She didn't have to say that she understood. She just ran into my arms, wrapping herself around my waist. I squeezed her gently back and relished in the moment. It had been a while since we actually hugged like this.

"Just don't leave me, okay? No matter how tough things get, don't leave without me."

"I won't." I whispered, my throat tightening.

"Promise me!"

I leaned down slightly, resting my chin on her head. "I promise I will not leave without you, Pearl."

I wanted to say the rest of the night was better. Pearl and I found the pens and worked on her poster together. She was creating a book report to present to her class. I had no idea what the book was about, no matter how many times she tried to explain it to me. But I found it adorable how passionate she was about her chosen book — that could not have been me. I hated reading and doing assignments, even though our homework was easy when we were in the program. We barely had any. It astonished me how smart Pearl was. She was the perfect little girl and the perfect student. I couldn't have been prouder.

I kind of wish the night had ended there, right after Pearl had gone to bed. I wish I wasn't an insomniac then I wouldn't have had to deal with Bexley. She came by my room around eleven, probably hearing my racing thoughts and wanting to clear the tension from earlier. That or she wasn't done screaming at me, and the second round was about to happen.

"What do you need now, Bexley?"

"I want to talk with you properly."

Yeah, right. She was definitely coming here for round two of screaming.

"Could we do this somewhere where we won't wake people up?"

"I'm being serious. I want to talk."

"And so am I. I'm not about to wake Pearl up with our screaming. She has a presentation tomorrow, it's the last thing she needs."

Why did she have to roll her eyes?

"Real mature, Bexley."

"Says the one assuming things."

"Okay, fine. What do you want to talk about then?"

"I was going to apologize and explain what's been going on, but you are just itching for a fight."

"Screw you. I'm not itching to fight you, I'm just tired and don't want to deal with you."

"That's too bad because we are going to talk."

Really? Why couldn't she just respect my wishes? I didn't want to talk right now. I didn't even want to see her.

"What do you want?" I snapped.

She hesitated. Just for a second. "I'm pregnant, okay?"

Holy shit.

No!

No way!

"What?" I blinked at her, sure I'd misheard. But her face stayed still. Unmoving. Dead serious.

"I've been off all week," she said, her voice shaky but firm. "And I took a test yesterday."

My stomach dropped. "You're serious?"

"Yes!" she snapped. "Of course, I'm serious!"

Holy shit!

My pulse picked up, thunder in my ears. I tried to steady my breath. "What are you going to do?"

Her brows furrowed like I'd just insulted her. "What do you mean? I'm keeping it."

I stared at her, stunned. "You're keeping it? Are you insane?"

Her eyes narrowed. "What is that supposed to mean? Of course, I would keep it."

"Bexley..." I sighed, trying to stay calm.

"Do you know what the government would do if they found out?"

She folded her arms over her chest, defensively. "Nothing, Sean! The program has been shut down. They can't do anything to me."

"I'm not talking about you." I took a step forward. "I'm talking about the fetus. For all we know, they could start up an entirely new program just for your child."

"They wouldn't do that," she said, but her voice lacked conviction now.

I saw the flicker of doubt in her eyes.

"How do you know? They tried to do it with Chip, what's stopping them from actually doing it now? Or even worse, what if they create a law that makes it so that we aren't allowed to have children."

"They wouldn't."

"You don't know that."

"Why aren't you thinking logically, Bexley?"

"I am!"

"You're not. You're just thinking about your future with that guy. Might I add, the guy who has no clue who you are!"

"Why does that matter?"

"You're joking? What happens when the government comes knocking and snatches your baby because you decided to have it? What are you going to tell your precious boyfriend then?"

I stepped closer, my voice low now, sharp as a blade. "Are you going to tell him all about who you truly are? Are you going to let him see the darkness in you?"

Silence.

"That's what I thought!" Her face tightened, but she didn't back down.

"I'm not going to get rid of it," she said sharply. "Nor let the government take my baby."

I stepped forward, heart pounding. "Bexley! You have to get rid of it. There's no way they aren't going to find out."

"I'm not getting rid of my child!"

"It's not even a baby yet! It's just cells!"

So much for us not yelling at each other. There we go waking up the entire house.

"I don't care!" she yelled, fists clenched. "It's mine, and I'm not letting anyone, or anything take it from me!"

"You're stupid then." I snapped. "Waverly can only protect you for so long and from so much. The government will end up taking it from you and probably putting it through what they did to us."

Her eyes searched mine, desperate. "How do you know?"

I couldn't stop. The words were already falling out, bitter and sharp.

"That's what they do!" I shouted. "They destroy the innocence of everything that isn't human and make them out to be something that they believe."

My voice dropped, low and steady. "They made us into monsters – or in our case, killers."

Bexley faltered, her arms hugging her stomach like she could shield it from the truth. "But you don't have evidence that it will happen."

"I don't need evidence. Just look at us! Look at everything we've been through! Look at Chip and Cory! You really want to risk putting a child through that! Putting your child through what happened with Chip!"

"No! But we don't know if it will happen!" she yelled, her voice trembling between desperation and defiance.

"But you don't know either!" I snapped, pacing across the room like I was trying to outrun the memory. "We didn't think it would happen with him, and it did! Now you are consciously choosing to endanger your child just because you want to have one! Fucking adopt one, then!"

Her eyes welled with tears, but she didn't look away. "Screw you, Sean! You know how miraculous this is! Plus, we don't even know if the baby will be like me!"

"We were made in a fucking lab!" I shouted, fists clenched. I wanted to punch or throw something, but refrained. "Chances are high that the child will end up exactly like you! You're still willing to risk it!"

"So what!" she screamed back, her voice cracking. "It's my body! My life! My choice!"

My jaw clenched. I couldn't look at her when I said it. "Then I will have no part in this."

The air in the room changed. Her voice broke. "What do you mean?"

"I'm leaving," I said coldly. "I won't stick around here and watch as you endanger its life because you're being selfish. I won't be a part of that!"

Her face fell. "Sean-"

"You can't force me to stay! You can't force me to be a part of its life, especially because you're endangering it. I can't be a part of that! I won't be!"

Even if I cared deeply about her, I wasn't ready to watch another person I loved get ripped away and put through hell. I couldn't do that. I had already had to watch it with Pearl. I wouldn't do it again.

I couldn't do it again.

"Sean?"

"Get out, Bexley! I cannot talk to you right now."

"Sean?" Her voice was softer this time, almost pleading.

"Bexley, I'm serious." My throat tightened. "Go!"

I didn't sleep that night. How could I? Everything happened too fast and I was struggling to keep up. Why did she have to keep it? Why did she want to keep it?

It made no sense.

But I kept true to my word. I wasn't going to stick around. I couldn't be a part of its life, not with her risking it. It wasn't fair.

I cared about her – hell, I loved her. She was my older sister! Yet I couldn't stay around when she ruined her life. Ruined the child's life just by having it.

It wasn't fair.

I was true to my word. I had to be.

Also, true to my word, I got two plane tickets to leave Florida. Pearl was coming with me as I promised. I wasn't going to leave her.

I knew she heard the argument from last night and thankfully, she said nothing, but I was truly leaving. It wasn't something I said in the heat of the moment.

I was leaving, and I was taking Pearl with me. End of story.

Or at least I thought it was.

Of course, Bexley had to come up to me as I packed and twisted a knife into my gut. Not physically, though I almost wish it was. At least then, it wouldn't have hurt as much as what she said.

"What do you think you're going to do? You go out there, ready to punch everything — everyone — in your path. That's not how things work anymore. You can't just rely on your strength, especially when it comes to raising her. You can't protect her out there. The only way to truly protect her is to leave her behind. That way, you were giving her the best chance of a life, one we could never have."

Why did she have to be right?

I was going to ruin Pearl's life if I took her with me, but the thought of leaving her made me sick.

I didn't want to leave her, but I couldn't stay.

I wanted to take her with me, but then I'd risk giving her a horrible, unstable life. I couldn't do that to her. I'd never forgive myself.

But what about my promise? I promised I wouldn't leave her. I meant it. I couldn't just leave her!

Fuck! Why was everything so complicated now? Why did life have to be so complicated?

I wanted to take her.

I should have taken her.

Yet, I listened to Bexley and left Pearl to stay there. Stay where she'd have a normal, stable life. One that I wouldn't ruin.

But at least I didn't just leave. I had to say goodbye.

"You're leaving me! Why? What did I do?" Her voice cracked, panicked. Her eyes were already glassy with tears.

"You promised to take me with you! You promised! Why are you breaking it? Why are you leaving me here?"

"Pearl, it's for the best."

Her fists clenched. She shook her head, violently. "I'm supposed to go with you! You said I would!"

"I'm sorry, Pearl. I can't take you. You need to stay here."

"Don't you dare leave me! Don't you dare walk out that door!"

"Pearl-"

"If you walk out, don't expect me to care about you anymore! Don't expect me to answer your calls!" She was trembling now. Her voice cracked with every word.

"If you walk out that door, forget me! Never think of me again! Don't even try to remember me!"

"Pearl, please?"

"If you're going to treat me like nothing, to go back on your promise, then I'm going to be nothing! I'm no one to you if you leave!"

My heart broke as she screamed after me. But there was no fighting it. I had to go. I had to leave.

"Sean! Don't leave me!"

"Please don't leave me!"

"Sean!"

I was protecting her. I was giving her a better chance at life. Giving her the chance I never had. I was protecting her — protecting her from me.

I would always protect her.

***

Ding.

"You killed my son, so now you can find her body at this location."

The address was somewhere around Kingswood Township. From the look of it, it was an abandoned old warehouse — the one that Damien had mentioned.

I had to get there before he did. Stop him from killing her.

Ding.

"You fucked with the wrong person, Sean Barnes. Now you're going to pay."

No, Mr. Crane! You fucked with the wrong person.

I was supposed to protect Pearl and give her a life better than mine. There was no way I'd let him ruin that. Ruin her chances of truly living.

Now it was his turn to understand who he was messing with.

Should have read the fine print.

Don't fuck with Sean Barnes.

UNTREATABLE PYROMANIA

I might have jumped the gun after receiving the address. I sped out of the city. Surprisingly I wasn't caught by any officers with how reckless I was driving. Not that I would've stopped to deal with them, my sister's life was on the line, and I couldn't waste time by being pulled over. Thankfully, it seems like luck was on my side.

Maybe I shouldn't have jumped the gun so soon. Because in my panic, I didn't properly punch the address into the GPS. I was driving blind because I didn't fully know how to get there. Eventually, I would have to stop for gas, so I could just do it then. I was becoming paranoid, though. What if, by not punching in the address, I was wasting more time and not taking the quickest route? What if I had already missed the turn-off to head in the direction it was? What if I was just wasting time, and she was already in fatal danger?

That's when my phone vibrated, cutting through the chaos in my mind like a blade.

Seriously? Who would be calling me at a time like this?

I glanced at the screen. I didn't recognize the number.

I snapped, and my grip tightened on the wheel. "Whoever the fuck this is, now is not the time!"

"Sean? Oh, thank god!"

My stomach dropped at the familiar voice.

"Bexley?" My voice came out quieter, strained with disbelief.

"Yeah, I'm so glad I could reach you! Do you know how worried I've been?"

I felt my pulse spike. Anger rushed in like wildfire. "Why have you been worried? Oh, maybe it's because you promised to protect and give Pearl a better life, and she's been fucking kidnapped!"

My voice cracked on the last word. Fury and panic twisting together in my chest like a barbed wire knot.

"Don't take that tone with me." Bexley snapped back. "I've been trying to help ever since she sent me that distressing message."

"Maybe someone should have been at the house with her, so she didn't have to send a distressing message!"

A beat of silence followed. "What do you mean? She hasn't been living with me for the past year."

Wait—what?

My grip on the wheel loosened for half a second. "What? Then who? Where?"

"She's been in California with Cory and Chip. Cory convinced me that it was a better and cooler place to raise a teenager, and Pearl agreed."

My jaw clenched so hard I thought a tooth might crack.

"Well, thanks for informing me!"

"I thought Mom or Pearl, or Cory would have told you."

"No! I haven't heard from Pearl or Cory in years, and I just started talking with Mom again. And let's just say the circumstances as to why I've been talking to Mom are not the best."

"Yeah, I heard. You've got yourself into quite a mess."

"Whatever, I'm just trying to do the right thing."

"Look where that's getting you. You're going after a notoriously violent man, who hires thugs to do his dirty work, and you're going alone. Come on, Sean, you're smarter than this."

Her words landed with more sting than I wanted to admit.

"I'm only worried about getting Pearl back safe and alive."

"Yet you're still doing this alone! You shouldn't be."

"So what, you going to fly over here to help me? Or are you just going to keep pestering me about my stupidity? Because I don't have much time for the latter."

"I'm not trying to pester you, I'm trying to get you to think logically. It's not working."

"No shit!"

"Okay, enough! I didn't call you to argue."

Now that was surprising.

"That's a shocker, you always would call me to yell. Are you sick?"

"Screw you! I'm not sick. I'm just trying to help you."

"Right? Help me. Even though you're in Florida, and I'm trying to find some abandoned warehouse in the middle of nowhere New Jersey."

"Had you punched it into your phone, you'd know where you were going."

"Have you been listening to my thoughts? Really? That's all kinds of messed up and creepy."

"Had I not been listening, then I couldn't have helped."

Almost on cue, my phone lit up, and the GPS was on. It showed me exactly where I needed to go and how soon I could get there.

"What the fuck?"

"You're welcome," Bexley said like she hadn't just hijacked my phone. "I've been talking to Mom and got her to put the GPS on for you. No need to thank me."

"I wasn't going to. It doesn't make up for your creepiness."

"Okay, well then this might. I have someone who will help you and is willing to fight to get Pearl back."

"Who's that?"

"You don't know him."

"I don't care, who is he?"

"He's just someone that Cory thought could help you, and he knows Pearl, he wants to help."

I stiffened, fingers tightening around the steering wheel.

"How does he know Pearl? Who is this guy?"

"Okay, calm yourself. They're just friends. They met at the police station."

My gut dropped.

"The police station! What?"

"Let's be honest, Pearl is no angel. Of course, she's had trouble with the law. She's your sister."

I felt like I'd been sucker-punched. First, I found out she wasn't even living with Bexley.

Now this? What the hell kind of brother was I?

"Anyway, they became best friends, and now she's been helping him go through his therapy and been going to addictions anonymous with him."

"What's he addicted to?"

"Sean? I don't-"

"Bexley, tell me. If you're forcing me to work with the guy, you need at least tell me about him."

"He's a pyro-" I slammed the brakes with my foot, just barely avoiding swerving off the road.

"You sent me a fucking arsonist!"

"Now, hold up-"

"Bexley, you best be kidding right now! I'm not about to put mine and Pearl's life in the hands of a pyromaniac!"

"He's getting better at controlling his impulses and not burning places to the ground." Fantastic. What an improvement.

"Is he gifted or superhuman?"

That's how you can tell the difference between those born in the facility versus those born with natural gifts. Bexley, Pearl, Tilly, me, and everyone else from the facilities were superhuman. We were given our talent — curse — through science and technology. People who are gifted, like Ayla, who I believe to be gifted, are born with subtle talents. There hasn't been much research on it, but the stuff that has been uncovered is that those who were born gifted descend from some magical ancestor — like a supernatural ancestor. It would make sense for Ayla to be one as she does come from a supernatural family, therefore she has magical ancestry.

"Does it matter?" Bexley's voice cut through my thoughts.

"It does."

The difference between gifted and superhuman wasn't just science—it was scale. Gifted individuals were soft and didn't pack a hard punch. They are rather gentle talents and have a limit to what they influence and how much can be influenced. Yet for superhumans, most, if not all of us, were made in labs. Our entire DNA was altered and manipulated – our abilities shoot out like bullets. Many people, if not trained properly, struggle to control their abilities.

"He's superhuman," Bexley admitted.

My stomach sank. "Makes sense why he's in therapy and going to addiction sessions."

"He's trying, okay? He didn't have what we did."

I scoffed, bitterness dripping from my words. "Ain't he a lucky son of a bitch then?"

"I mean, he didn't have the support we did. He wasn't trained to understand his ability."

Of course, he wasn't. Another unstable livewire just waiting to go off. "So you sent me an amateur superhuman who is impulsive and an arsonist. If you wanted me dead, you could have just said that."

"Sean, be serious!"

"I am! This guy might end up killing me by accident because he let his emotions take the reins, and he exploded."

"Don't be so pessimistic, have faith in the guy."

"Have faith in a guy I've never met? No thanks."

"Okay, let me rephrase. Give him a chance, he might just surprise you."

"Yeah, surprise me with fire. Can't wait to die that way."

"Sean."

"Bexley." Our usual rhythm. Always bickering. Always circling the real issue.

"Be nice. He wanted to help. He cares about Pearl too."

That part stopped me — but only for a second. "Okay, whatever. If he makes even the tiniest flame without me telling him to, I'm benching him. In other words, I'm knocking him out and locking me in the trunk of my car. Got it?"

"Yeah, alright. Just be nice."

"Uh-huh."

"Are we done talking now, Bexley?"

"I guess so."

"Oh. Wait. Sean?"

"Yes, Bexley?"

"Go get our sister back safe and sound!"

"I will."

"Oh, and Sean?"

"Yes, Bexley?"

"Make them all pay for fucking with us."

"It would be my pleasure."

It's a common occurrence for us not to say goodbye. 'Goodbye' to us was a way of showing a lack of confidence. 'Goodbye' was almost like saying we weren't gonna make it out. None of us said goodbye unless we had no faith in ourselves or believed the mission was too dangerous for us to succeed. We'd never say goodbye unless we had to.

I wasn't going to say goodbye this time.

I was getting my sister back one way or another.

This mission would be successful no matter what. No matter if I didn't make it in the end.

My focus was only to save Pearl. Not myself.

Her life was worth way more than mine, and I would do anything in my power to keep her alive.

No matter what, Pearl was getting out of there.

Maybe I should have said goodbye.

True to my word, I gave the guy a chance. By that, I mean I wanted to meet up with him to see if he was worth coming with me. That was my first mistake.

We met at a diner just off the highway.

Susanne's Diner.

I think that's what it was called, but don't quote me. It was something along those lines.

He was exactly how you'd expect a pyromaniac to dress — or at least how I expected him to dress. My guess is he wanted to look cool as he wore a leather jacket and black ripped jeans. I can already tell you he did not look cool. He looked like a rebellious teenager trying to get attention and trying to look like a bad boy. I picked him out of everyone in the diner because he was exactly what I imagined. There was no way in hell I was gonna let him help me, dressed like that.

"Yo, you big bro, Sean?"

I shouldn't have slid into this booth. There was no way in hell I was gonna be able to deal with him, especially not if he talked like that all the time.

"Lose the gangster persona."

"Whoa, bro, we're all cool here."

Yep, I've had it. I tried to give him a chance. There was no way he'd survive a car ride with me. I'd murder him on the drive out. I can't with the fake bullshit talk.

"Alright, enough. Bexley told me you wanted to help, and the only way that's happening is if you cut the bullshit persona."

"Bro, this is how-"

"Okay, okay, hold up! I'll stop."

It took me standing up to get him to drop it, kind of sad if you ask me.

"I talk like that so people can respect me."

"Nobody is going to respect you if you talk like that. They're going to think you're dumb and don't know how to communicate properly."

"Okay, ouch."

"Besides, you're a wielder of fire. Why would you talk like that to gain respect?"

"Dude, be quiet. I don't want people to know."

"What did you do?"

"I didn't do anything."

"Yeah, right. If you're going to be coming with me, you have to be completely honest with me, or else this isn't going to work. You're still a child in the eyes of the law, and I'm now in charge of you."

"Whoa, we're just getting Pearl back. Nothing more."

I didn't answer. He didn't understand — not yet. This wasn't just some rescue mission.

"I need to know if people are coming after you. People as in the authorities."

"People are always after me, been in and out of jail more times than I can count."

He waved down the waitress mid-confession like this was just a casual hangout.

"Oh, miss. Can I get some waffles and a chocolate shake? You want anything, big bro?"

"I'm fine."

"Just those, then."

Why was he winking at the waitress? Who did he think he was? Girls don't fall for shit like that anymore, so why was he trying? Don't get me started on what he ordered, either. It was like he was purposely trying to behave like a child and yet he tried to flirt with the waitress. Yeah, good luck with that one, buddy. Did you want her to cut up the waffles for you while she was at it?

"Are you in trouble now?"

"Depends who you ask."

What's with the cryptic responses? We didn't have time for this.

"Seriously?"

"Well, I don't think I'm in trouble, but the few cars I left burning in California might get me in trouble with the cops."

"Are you kidding me?"

I'm potentially working with an active arsonist. Lucky fucking me!

"Cool it. Nobody knows where I was headed." Of course, he thinks he's smarter than law enforcement.

"Except, you're the number one suspect, as I'm guessing you ditched your parole officer. And there are cameras all over the country, so your face is pretty recognizable."

"I don't think it's that recognizable."

"Oh, you don't! Well, I'm guessing you didn't think about the numerous mugshots you had to take going in and out of jail. Chances are pretty high that you're being actively looked for as we speak."

"I mean, probably not."

"I'm sure. But by all means, wait for your order of waffles and the chocolate shake. We have all the time in the world — oh wait. We actually don't!"

"I don't need the disappointed dad treatment."

"Good, because I'm way beyond disappointed dad. I'm going to give you ten seconds to get out of here and into my car, or else I'm leaving you for the authorities."

"Yeah, because that's not a disappointed dad right there."

"What did you say?"

"Nothing. I'm going. I'm going."

In true child fashion, he stomped out of the diner as if he was having a tantrum. This is why I don't normally associate myself with children. Meanwhile, I had to go pay for the child's order, not that it was too expensive. And lucky me, I got our waitress at the register.

"Hey, I'm really sorry. My friend didn't realize how much of a hurry we were in and ordered food. I'm just going to pay for it and then head out. Maybe you could just give it to the hitchhiker I saw standing outside. I figure he's probably hungry."

She seemed to believe my explanation and handed me the receipt.

That little shit!

I assumed he had only gotten the waffles and the chocolate shake. Boy, was I wrong? That fucking kid left me with a bill that was worth almost two hundred dollars. What did he even order before I got there?

This is what I get for trying to be nice.

That fucking kid!

"You're really sweet, ya know. Paying for the bill like that and giving me a good tip."

"Yeah, yeah. I'm a real saint."

A real saint who got conned by a kid.

Not only was he an arsonist, but he was a con artist too. Fan-fucking-tastic!

"Please come again! Oh, and here."

She handed me a folded piece of paper with a few numbers on it.

You've got to be shitting me! Did his attempts really work on her?

"You want me to give it to the kid?"

Oh, she got shy quickly. Damn! Her face is beet red. I almost felt bad for asking. Who am I to judge her for liking the attention he was giving?

Maybe I shouldn't have said anything and just left with the paper.

"It's for you."

Oh.

Oh!

What?

"Oh- OH! Thank you." I guess?

That changed the mood real quick.

I think I was blushing now.

I should go.

I really should go.

"Well, I'll see you around."

Real smooth, Sean. Real smooth.

Just don't embarrass yourself while you leave. I'd never live that down.

Geez.

That was shocking.

"Dude, what took you so long?"

"Just get in the fucking car."

"Pushy, pushy. Why didn't Pearl tell me these stories about you? You're an asshole."

"She talks about me?"

Why would she talk about me? I abandoned her.

I thought she hated me.

Why did that make me feel all warm inside? I still left her, and just because she wasn't talking bad about me, didn't mean she missed me. I shouldn't read into his comments.

"First things first about this mission, you will listen to everything I say. No flames will happen unless I say so. Got it?"

"Alright, buzzkill."

I had to ignore that comment or else I would have pushed him onto the freeway.

"Secondly, that outfit has got to go. I have some kevlar in the back of my car that might fit you, but there's no way you're going into this dressed like that."

"Dude, respect the fit!"

"I have no respect for a wannabe gangster."

"Ouch. Your words hurt."

"Thirdly, if things start getting out of hand, I want you to get the hell out of there. I will not be the reason your young life ends."

"What about Pearl?"

"If you can get to her safely, then do it. If not, don't risk it. You're new to this whole thing, I didn't expect you to know how missions like these go."

"Do you?"

"Do I what?"

"Know how these missions go. I mean, Pearl told me about what you used to do."

"Your point?"

"Have you ever done a rescue mission before?"

"A few times, but they weren't what you'd expect."

"Tell me about them."

"No. I don't know you."

"And I don't know you, yet I still got in your car."

"You make a good point."

"Are you going to tell me?"

"How about we make a deal? I tell you one of the rescue missions I was on and you tell me about yourself. Sound fair?"

"Yeah, yeah. Spill!"

"You know us being assassins, but you don't know what that fully entails. There were moments where even law enforcement would hire us to help out the situations, like torturing someone for information."

"That's sick!"

No, it wasn't. It was corrupt and twisted.

"One of my colleagues was chosen to go get information on the cartel in Texas. Rather than getting information they ended up getting captured by the people they were supposed to interrogate. Our mom, Waverly, planned a rescue mission to get them back, and I was a part of the team. Long story short, a fight broke out, and several of my colleagues didn't make it, but neither did half of the cartel. It was kind of a win-win in a way."

No, it really wasn't. I lost some of my closest friends during that mission because we underestimated the people we were against. We were young and new to the program. Due to the abilities we had we thought we were unstoppable and able to conquer the world. That wasn't true. We ended up being just as vulnerable as a human, if not more, with our cockiness. Because of it, we lost five of our own. Five!

Of course, this mission happened before we were given our custom clothing and indestructible suits. I think it was one of the reasons Waverly decided to invest and design the clothing pieces, to avoid more causalities. Even though it really didn't stop much.

The remaining people who survived the rescue mission — excluding me — were gone now. They didn't make it past the program shutting down. Everything piled up for them, and they only saw one way out. It sucked. I hated that they couldn't have the freedom that we were given after the program shut down, but I guess, in a way, they found their own freedom.

"We were cocky and got ourselves killed during the mission. It just sucks that the person we were trying to save ended up dead as well. But you live, and you learn."

I hated how emotionless I sounded. It was almost like I wasn't even human as I spoke those words. It was almost like they were programmed into my brain, and I wasn't allowed to feel anything over the death of my friends.

They were my friends! I should be allowed to cry and feel sad over their deaths! I should be allowed to feel shame over our fuck up! Then why didn't I sound like I was upset? Why didn't I allow myself to feel that sadness?

"That's horrible. I'm sorry that happened to you."

Nobody had ever said sorry to me about the things I went through. Waverly and the rest of my family are always around to comfort me, but none of them ever said sorry. It was strange hearing it, yet there was comfort in hearing it, too. Maybe this guy wasn't so bad after all. Or perhaps he was trying to get brownie points for me? Either way, I appreciate his apology for the trauma I went through, even if he wasn't involved.

"Thank you. You're one of the first people to say that to me."

"It's funny, Pearl said the same thing."

"Guess you two are truly siblings."

I thought we were having a moment, but then he had to go and ruin it by making a dumb comment like that. Obviously, we were biological siblings, if our appearance wasn't the dead giveaway, our mannerisms definitely did.

"Your turn."

"Well, my life isn't as exciting as yours-"

I wouldn't go that far to say my life was exciting.

Traumatizing would be a better word for it.

"My name is Finley O'Hara Gomez — I know, crazy name — but I go by Flint for short."

"You're a pyrokinetic that goes by Flint?"

"I know it's a sick name!"

Right...

"Anyway, I was born to two loving people, Brian O'Hara and Brandon Gomez. Okay, well not born from their genes, but they adopted me. Apparently, someone abandoned me at a firehouse-"

Ironic.

"-and that's where Brandon worked at the time. After some much-needed communication with his husband, they ended up taking me in and adopting me."

"How sweet. You had a loving family to grow up with."

"I can hear the sarcasm in your voice, and it's really rude."

Obviously, there was sarcasm in my voice. This kid was a genetically made human, and yet he wasn't forced to grow up in a facility. He has a loving family. How was that fair?

"I'm sorry, please continue."

"When I was three, they adopted little Robbie and his twin sister, Rosalyn. From there, I became the older brother, the one who had to protect his siblings. Like you. Only they weren't like me at all."

He shouldn't have compared us like that. He wasn't like me at all.

"I started discovering I was different around the age of five. I always had a fascination for flames, and one day, I got too curious and stuck my hand into the fireplace. Keep in mind this was an actual fireplace, not one of those fancy electric ones. It didn't hurt, I stuck my hand in the fire, but I do remember Brian screaming and rushing over to rip my hand out of there. Only I had no damage on my hand. I wasn't burnt or anything."

"One of the pros of being a pyrokinetic."

"Why do you keep calling me that?"

"That's what you are? You're able to manipulate and create fire. That's what they are called."

"It sounds scientific. But still, how do you know what it's called? We just met."

"You're not the first PK I've met. One of my closest friends was like you."

"Really? Do you think he could help me?"

"She. And no. She's been gone for a few years now."

"Oh. That's shitty."

Tell me about it, kid. She was one of my closest friends in both the facility and the program. She was adopted by one of Waverly's many family members, and though she too made it out of the program, she later succumbed to the trauma. She overdosed one night on fluff – I want to believe she wasn't intentionally trying to pass that night. She was one of the only dead people I ever cried for, I think. Maybe it was because the program had shut down, and I could actually properly mourn the loss of my friend.

"Long story short, I kept trying and trying to experience what I did at the fireplace but my fathers kept a strict eye on me. It wasn't until I was like ten that I found Brian's lighter. He used to be a smoker before and eventually stopped after I entered the picture, but he still kept the lighter around. Anyway, I got a hold of it and started seeing what I can do."

"That's cool. You got to understand your ability without any pressure."

"I wouldn't say it was good. I ended up burning the house down when I was twelve. Thankfully nobody was in the house at the time, other than me. Or at least that's what I thought. But, I didn't burn. I wasn't even crispy."

It was easy to see where the story was going.

"You don't have to say anymore. I won't force you to relive that."

"No! I need to. My therapist says it's good to find triggers and not explode when they happen, though I don't think she knows that when I mean explode, I mean it literally."

"Please don't explode me and my car?"

"I'll try not to."

"I didn't know that Brandon had come back into the house for something. They were supposed to be at family friend's birthday. He wasn't supposed to be there. My - my dad didn't make it out of the fire, but I did. I had to turn myself over to the authorities. I didn't think I was safe being out there – being loose. I told them about how it was an accident. I was just playing around with the lighter and caught the curtains on fire, but it got out of control. Just kept getting bigger and bigger the more I panicked. And then there were Brandon's screams, he was trying to get to me, but got trapped by the flames. It was my fault — even if the rest of my family didn't blame me. I'm the reason my dad is dead. I shouldn't have been playing with the lighter. But either way, the cops took my statement and gave me a few weeks in juvie. I wasn't there long enough."

"Damn! I don't know what to say." I wanted to reach out to him, maybe even give him a little pat. Something to show that I understood what he felt. But I didn't.

"Don't say sorry. I've heard too many people say that."

"Trust me, I wasn't going to give you pity."

"Really?"

"I mean, yeah, it sucks that you ended up killing your dad, but it wasn't fully your fault. Impulsivity often controls our actions and always controls our abilities. You were a child, who wanted to play around with fire, you wouldn't be the first one. I mean, not all children end up killing their fathers, but still. Not all children are like us. Plus, there's a bright side to your story."

"Oh yeah? How's that?"

"You weren't charged with murder, only arson. That's got to count for something."

"You know, you're a really fucked up person, Sean."

"Thank you. I've been told that many times."

I've told myself that many times. I was a fucked up, twisted person. I saw the slightest amount of positivity in some twisted shit and brought it out into the light for others to see. What could I say? I was a killer with a sociopathic personality.

"I didn't mean it really as a compliment."

"I know, but I don't really care."

"So now you know who I am. Ever since my first charge, I've been in and out of jail for the same charges. I am an arsonist, as you said, or a pyromaniac. And I haven't really seen my other dad or siblings. I can't stand the look on their faces when they see me."

"Don't think of the names as a bad thing, they just give you more character."

"You think?"

"Oh yeah! Flint, the arsonist, sounds like a real badass. People should be scared of him."

I'm glad I could make him laugh by saying that. He seemed like he needed a good laugh. Plus, I didn't like the weird tension that was in the car, it would have made for an awkward rest of the drive.

"Thank you, Sean. I can see why Pearl looked up to you."

"Hey now! Don't go soft on me now. We got some asses we need to kick, and I need Flint, the arsonist here."

"I wasn't going soft! I was just saying thank you!"

"You don't need to thank me. You could have left it at that."

"But you need to know my appreciation for understanding my past."

"You don't need to thank me. We all have pasts that we are ashamed of. I don't need you to be appreciative of my understanding of trauma."

That's all I really knew. Trauma this and trauma that.

"Okay. Fine! I'm going to be the tough arsonist, Flint, and I'll never thank you again!"

"Now that's the spirit!"

<hr>

"So, what's our plan of attack?"

"Well, we know where they're gonna be taking her, so I think taking out as many guards as we can and grabbing her. That's the only plan we need."

"How'd you know where they were taking her?"

"The guy who took her texted me, saying where they would be putting her body. And it's at this building."

"What do you mean?"

"He told me he was taking her?"

"But you said, taking her body. Is she dead? Are you making us find her body?"

"No! Previously, this guy mentioned how much my mother was willing to pay to get us back, so there was no way he was gonna kill us. Kill her! He's trying to lead me into a trap."

"Why would Waverly want to get you back?"

"Not Waverly, our biological mother. That psychopath."

"Oh. And you're sure of all this?"

"Of course I am, no matter what I've done, he still wants to get paid."

"How are you so sure?"

"Because it's what any of us would've done in the past. Plus, if he really wanted to kill her, why would he go through making me come to her body? If he was really gonna kill her, he would've dropped her off at my doorstep or sent me packages of bits of her. I know that this is a trap."

It had to be a trap. It just had to be.

"If this is a trap, then what makes you think she's going to be there?"

"Because she's the bait. She has to be here."

"So, in other words, you don't actually know if she's going to be dead or not, and you're going off of some instinct that this is all just a trap?"

"Yep! And you're going to help me."

"Fantastic, you're actually insane."

"From what I can see, this is an old pipeline or mining warehouse that hasn't been used in years because somewhere there's a gas leak, and it reeks of gas. We're going to sneak in and grab my sister. Hopefully, we will not have to deal with any of those men, but we will if we have to. Then you'll blow it up."

"What?"

"What part was unclear?"

"You said that the only plan we needed was to get her and now you're expecting me to blow up a building? That doesn't make any sense."

"Of course it doesn't, but if you ask me, it's a really good plan."

"I'm not saying it isn't. I'm just confused why you didn't say that before."

"I didn't think I needed to get into much detail about how we were going to get my sister back, but I guess I had to."

"So am I blowing this building up with the guys inside still, or how is that going to go down? What happened to fighting the guys too?"

"You won't be fighting any of them, and preferably the guys would still be inside, but if they're not, I can take care of them."

Preferably they would all be dead before the building was blown up, but I wasn't too picky on how they died. Though I would try my hardest to get less blood on Flint's hands.

"I want it to seem like they were checking out the building, and it accidentally combusted."

"Uh-huh."

"That way, no one would come looking for any suspects. Sounds like a win-win to me."

"I know I said this earlier, but you are a sick bastard Sean. I don't know if it's a good thing."

"That's okay, one of us needs to have a twisted side, and judging by your age and lack of experience in this department, I guess it's gotta be me. Don't worry, none of their blood will be on your hands. I'll make sure of it."

"Am I supposed to be comforted by that?"

"No, but it's the truth. I already have enough blood on my hands might as well just add a bit more. You, on the other hand, don't have any. I want to keep it that way."

Well, not actual blood on his hands, more like ash.

"How nice of you?"

"Don't worry, if all things go as planned, we will be driving away from a giant fire the next time we get in this car. With my sister, of course."

"And hopefully, we're not going to find her body, like whoever that guy was suggested."

"Trust me. There's no way in hell we're gonna find her body. She's alive. I know it."

She was alive.

That is something I knew to be true.

Thank you, Waverly. I appreciate you putting the clothing on our backs and giving me access to monitor Pearl's health and location.

She was alive, and I was going to get her back no matter how many lives I took to do so.

DEADLY ALLEGIANCE

I never thought that this was where I'd end up at this point in the year. I figured maybe I'd have a job, and maybe I'd stop giving into my addictions, but never this. Then again, I promise I would never think of her, so of course, I never thought this would be how things turned out. It's crazy how one simple event could alter the future so extremely. It almost reminds me of this one saying that there's a point in your life where everything you've ever done and experienced, would come back and you'd be ready for it. It ended with some bullshit about how your previous lived experience would influence how you work out the problem – or something like that. I'm not sure who said that but I want to punch them in the face too. I didn't want everything that I had experienced —every life that I took — to be represented in this moment. Hell, I didn't want that one rescue mission to be represented now. I wasn't ready for the possibility that she might not make it out of this. I couldn't think that. If anyone wasn't going to make it out, it'd be me.

Pearl and Flint still had so much that they needed to experience in the world. They hadn't quite lived. They were still young, and though they had seen enough trauma to last a lifetime, they hadn't seen the beauty in the world. They hadn't traveled, tried exotic foods, or experienced any culture. They had to see the world and I would make sure of that.

I would make sure that the two of them got out of there alive. They deserved it way more than I did. Despite everything in their pasts, they still were innocent and deserved to have it preserved. I would do that for them.

I just wanted to be the big brother I was supposed to be. For once, I want to be the hero and not the killer I was born to be. I want Pearl to finally have the brother she deserved the one who is willing to do everything in his power to make sure she could go on. The big brother she could actually look up to. One that deserved her praise. I had to be that person for her, no matter what it took.

I guess the person was right with their saying, everything I had experienced was coming down to this one moment, and I was going to put it to good use. This, however, would be my last experience — I wasn't planning on getting out of there alive. I wasn't also planning on letting any of Crane's men or Mr. Crane get out of there alive. Why should they deserve to live after everything they put my sister through? After all they had done to those they kidnapped? Pearl was innocent in this whole mess, yet they still dragged her in and threatened her. They weren't going to make it by the end of this. That was a promise.

"How do you wear clothes like these? They are so uncomfortable!"

I wasn't lying when I said he had to change. The Kevlar was fire-resistant and would be more breathable if he needed to sweat.

"Of course, I've never worn those before. They are pretty much rock hard, you'll have to stretch them out before we go in."

"Now tell me, what did you see?"

"Okay, so there's three vans parked on the east side of the building, and from what I could see nobody is guarding the south entrance on the outside."

I had Flint do a perimeter check. I wanted him to have an idea of what to look for and what he should pay attention to. If I wasn't planning on getting out of here, I wanted Pearl to have someone properly equipped and knowledgeable about these things. She was bound to run into more problems like this in the future, and I wanted her to have a reliable partner. Plus, he's younger than me, and his bones don't crack when he runs. Sue me for using the young guy to do the physical exercise! Not to mention, he had to break into his Kevlar outfit. The only way to do that was to get him moving around in it – especially by jogging around and getting information.

But mainly because he was younger. I didn't need to run around and sweat when I had him to do it.

"But who's to say there isn't someone on the inside waiting."

"Fair point. There are at least four guys at the East entrance, all fully armed. Maybe two on the North side door, they are also armed, but not as heavily. And two more on the West side, who also aren't armed heavily."

"But the South side is unguarded?"

"Externally, yes."

"That's definitely a trap. He's counting on me taking the easy-looking door because it's clear outside — but there'll be six guys waiting just inside. Classic move. But Mr. Crane's not exactly a genius."

"Do we go to either of the doors with fewer men?"

"He might expect that too. Make it seem like he has fewer men guarding one door, yet still monitors those doors. Did you see any cameras around any of the doors?"

"I don't think so. Maybe?"

"What did I say about details?"

"Look at everything, even if it's the smallest thing there is. All details are important and can open your mind to the enemy's plans."

"Exactly! So were there any cameras?"

"Yes? I think there were two. One on the East and one on the West. I don't know specifically if it was a camera, but I remember seeing the faintest glint of red light when I was watching the men on the East."

"Good. Good job, Flint."

"What else?"

"This building should have been shut down by the DHS way faster than it was."

"What do you mean?"

"The second floor barely has any windows and if people were working with compressed gas, that's not good. Especially if one of those things burst and the room filled with gas, they'd have no way of airing it out properly. And don't get me started on the stairs that come down from the roof. That's a hazard in itself. There's no way more than one person would be able to get down those stairs, plus they're covered with boxes and stuff. It's limiting the space even more."

"There's roof access? Any men or cameras there?"

"Not that I could see, but once again, those stairs are a hazard. I doubt they'd even hold a person now from how rusted and busted they are."

"I wish I could get a blueprint of this building."

"Why?"

"Crane wouldn't risk putting his men up there out in the open or fully away from the others just in case they needed backup. Maybe at the bottom of the stairs inside the building is where he'd put them? It could be our point of entry."

"How so?"

"We could cause a distraction at one of the sides, then make our way up to the roof. Because there'd be a commotion at the side, if there are men by the stairs, they'll go to aid the other guys."

"I thought you wanted to be inconspicuous? Wouldn't the distraction defeat the whole point?"

"You're right. Then we can still try and sneak up the stairs and get access into the building from the roof. But we'll have to be careful, multiple doors lead to the roof, and we want to go through the door that has fewer, if not any men."

"Sounds easier said than done."

"Of course, but I have faith in our abilities. We've got this."

"Did I forget the mention that the stairs barely had a pathway?"

"You said that."

"And you still want us to go up them?"

"Yeah! We just have to step carefully and move with precision. We've got this."

"Where is this confidence coming from? Can you share?"

"One thing you need to know when on missions is to believe in your plans. If you think nervously, you'll end up being nervous, and then things will go wrong. You can't afford to have things go wrong when people's lives are on the line."

"Essentially, fake it until you make it."

"What? What does that even mean?"

"You've never heard that saying."

"No! What are you sixty-five or something? No kid like yourself says things like that."

"It's essentially what you just said in a short form. And plenty of people say it who aren't old as shit."

"I'm sorry, Flint. Nobody my age or younger would ever say that. You sure you're sixteen?"

"Shut up! Let's get inside."

"Good attempt at changing the subject, but we'll come back to this."

"I'm not changing the subject, I just want to get the tricky part over with so that we can get Pearl back faster."

"Ok, fine. Let's do this."

Flint wasn't wrong, this would probably be the trickiest part of the plan. Sneaking into the building without being seen or heard was going to be difficult. But I was going to let Flint do the stairs first. In that case, if any issues arose, he'd be out of the fight, and I could take care of whatever got thrown my way without having to worry about him. Plus, he was probably going to be a lot more stealthier than me — it really wasn't my specialty.

"Up you go. I'll follow right after you, I just need you to be almost at the top before I come. And if anything happens down here, don't worry about me. Just worry about getting Pearl."

"Do you think something is going to happen down here?"

"What? No! Of course not."

I couldn't make him nervous. I had to have total and complete confidence in him. That way, he'd feel the same about himself and would be more comfortable with potential situations that required him to use his ability. He just needed confidence in himself.

"Hey Flint, look at me."

Not to sound weird or creepy, but he had nice eyes.

Totally didn't sound creepy at all.

"Flint, I believe in you. You've got this. Just trust in yourself."

"Yeah."

"You've got this. Don't overthink it."

"Okay. I've got this."

"You've got this!"

"Now go and be that really cool dude. Who is he again? Who are you?"

"I'm Flint, the arsonist! I've got this!"

"Now, climb those stairs."

Sometimes people, especially children and teenagers, need that boost of confidence. Someone to tell them what they are doing is right, and they should be proud of themselves. I would gladly be that person for Flint at this moment. He needed someone to believe in him — someone to be proud of who he was. He was a pyrokinetic and an arsonist, but that didn't make him a bad guy. He wasn't a bad guy, he just didn't have the training that any of us did. Despite that, I was still proud of him, and I would be proud of him. I would be the person to boost his confidence that person to show him to not be afraid of who he was. He had control, he just needed someone to show him that he had it.

Maybe I spoke too soon.

It wasn't his fault how unstable the stairs were, but one of the boxes that were stacked on the stairwell began to wobble the higher Flint climbed. It was like a wooden crate or box, I'm not entirely sure. It was much higher above me, but it was stacked on two other boxes, so no doubt it would be the one to fall. Lucky for both Flint and I, as it finally tipped off the other two and let gravity take its course by falling towards me, I caught it. For anyone who wasn't like me, chances are the box would have shattered the bones in the person's forearms. Not me, though. One of the perks of my ability, my bones are stronger than most, and it took a lot of force to break them.

"Keep going. It was a minor inconvenience, not something worth stopping for."

Flint just had to continue climbing. He was almost at the top anyway, so there was no point in stopping now.

"Come on. You've got this, Flint."

Not that I think he heard me as I spoke softly. At this point, he was too high for me to properly talk to him, and I wasn't about to yell, giving away our position. Besides, I don't think Flint needed my encouragement as much anymore, he was doing alright without it. However, now I think about it, I'm pretty sure he has a fear of heights. It would explain his apprehension about going to the roof and why he was white knuckle gripping the railing. Originally, I just thought he was nervous, but now seeing as he won't look down, Flint was afraid of heights. I guess my encouragement and faux confidence helped him in more ways than one, or at least I think so. But that would also mean that I could not rely on him to give me the go-ahead for when he reached the top of the stairwell, as chances are he wasn't about to look down for me. So I guess that would be my time to climb. Hopefully, those boxes don't tumble down again, that's the last thing we needed.

"How was the climb for you?"

I made it up the stairs in record time after Flint and thankfully the other two boxes on the edge of the stairs did not move as I climbed. Then again, I wasn't holding onto the railing like Flint was and disturbing where they were resting. Again, the box falling was not Flint's fault. It could have happened to anyone or at any point.

"The stairs were so shaky and I'm pretty sure every step I took, there was a groaning."

"That's funny. I didn't hear anything."

"You flew up those stairs, I doubt your feet even touched any step."

"Please, flying isn't my ability. Plus, I hit almost every step just like you."

"Uh-huh. I'm sure you did."

"Oh, whoa. Look at that view. You know, if these circumstances were different, I'd say this is a beautiful place to look over the countryside. Wouldn't you agree?"

"Totally. A hundred percent agree."

Flint's back was to the ledge and he was focused more on the fire exit door that we would soon have to enter. I guess my observations were correct. Flint was definitely afraid of heights.

"You know, you could have told me that you didn't like being up high. I could have found an alternate way of getting in."

"And risk being caught or them knowing we're here. I can suck this up for a few minutes."

"Well, I'm glad you did this. You did good, and that box falling wasn't your fault."

Do you know how many times I wished someone would say that to me? Especially when it came down to doing my job. For whatever reason, someone chose me to kill their competitor, but it wasn't my fault that they chose me. It wasn't my fault that the person died. It wasn't my fault I was just doing a job. I know it's horrible of me to say especially with how much Waverly done for me, but I still wish she would've said it.

"Thank you. I was really trying to convince myself that I was in control."

"I could tell. You did good, and I could barely hear you climbing those stairs, which means nobody else heard. You did good, kid."

"Whoa! Don't start calling me 'kid' now. I'm a man, remember? Flint the arsonist."

"I'm so sorry, how could I forget."

He punched me lightly in the shoulder and chuckled. It was almost crazy how easily we got along together. It felt like I had known Flint for years, like I was an older brother figure to him. It's crazy how instantly clicked together.

Why did it make me feel tense and guilty? Almost like I shouldn't be feeling this way. I didn't know the guy fully, meaning I shouldn't trust him. Sure, he knew Pearl. But that didn't mean much. He could've barely known her, and yet here I was, trusting him to help me get her back. What if he was the reason she got taken in the first place? What if he helped Mr. Crane take her? I didn't know this guy. So why was I letting him punch me as if we had been friends for years? Why was I acting like an older brother to him?

I didn't know him.

I couldn't trust him.

"Where do we go from here?"

Could I trust him? Should I trust him?

"How long have you known my sister?"

I felt guilty asking questions, but I couldn't stop the destructive obsession forming in my thoughts.

"What?"

"Please, Flint. Just answer the question."

"You can't be serious? Not now. Not after everything we've talked about."

"Flint."

"No. You can't just switch up on me like this. I'm not the bad guy here. I'm not with those people."

I felt guilty. He knew exactly why I was asking the question too.

"I would never do this to Pearl. She's the only family who understands me. Please? I'm not a bad guy."

I've never seen a teenage boy breakdown so quickly, it hurt me. My chest squeezed knowing that I was the cause of this. I didn't have a moment to properly think over what I was about to do as I wrapped my arms around him.

"I'm sorry. I'm fucked in the head, and there are moments where I have to question everything and everyone. I want to trust you, I do. I just can't fully."

"Pearl was the first person to look at me like I wasn't a problem. She was there when no one else was. I'd never hurt her or betray her. I'd never do that to her family."

"I'm sorry. I'm sorry that I got her into this."

Yeah. I felt like a shitty person.

Look at me making a sixteen-year-old breakdown. I'm a horrible person. A shitty person.

"Let's go get her back, okay?"

I should've felt disgusted as he sniffled into my shirt and gently nodded his head without lifting it from my chest. I had never been this close to someone in several years — always avoiding any form of physical contact with anyone. Yet here I was, the one who initiated the hug and letting this kid cry into me. I think we both needed this moment. Just some time to fully process what we were about to do and pray that it would work out in our favor. If that means holding onto this kid a little longer and letting him cry on my shirt, then I guess I would let it happen.

In that moment, he felt like the little brother I never had — or maybe the one I lost. He wasn't just that to me, though. He was like a little brother to Pearl too. And suddenly, I understood why she stayed by his side, why she helped him the way she did.

She was doing exactly what I'd always tried to teach her: to look out for others, to protect those who needed it. I never thought she listened — not really. She used to roll her eyes every time I brought it up. But maybe that was her way of telling me she already understood. That she didn't need me to guide her. And that she didn't need reminders.

"You're a lot alike, you know."

I almost didn't hear him as he mumbled into my chest. I never expected to be compared to my little sister. She was innocent, kind, and I was, well I was just me. A perfected killer who enjoyed torturing people for information, being sarcastic and full of attitude all the time. I couldn't see how anyone could compare us. We were two very different people in my eyes. It should have been seen the same in other's eyes as well.

"Let's go get our sister back."

⁓

Mr. Crane's layout of his henchman? His workers? Or whatever they are, was exactly how I expected it to be. None of them were in the stairwell that led up to the roof, but positioned outside of, what I'm guessing they thought was the main door, were two of his men. Unannounced to them, there were multiple doors to get into the stairwell as it was a part of the emergency escape measures for the building. So many buildings like this one during the time they were made all had the same emergency escape plan — have multiple entrances to one main exit and deal with the risks later. It was an idiotic system and probably resulted in lives lost when danger struck. There wasn't any doubt in my mind that this place never faced danger. They dealt with compressed gas, so obviously, there was danger around the corner. Flint was right about this place though; the DHS would definitely fail this place if it were still up and running. Also, I could see what Damien meant about this place reeking of gas. The scent of sulfur and methane assaulted my senses as soon as we entered the room, I'm not entirely sure how anyone would be able even to stand in here for so long. All the more reasons to get my sister and get out.

"Here. This will help you breathe a bit better."

I always wanted to be prepared, then again I was supposed to be prepared, especially when it came to assignments. It was no shock that I pulled out some tiny masks that could attach to an oxygen canister in my bag.

"We have to be smart about how much oxygen we take from the can. If we use it all up now, we won't be prepared for a fight. Only take an inhale if you feel like you're going to pass out, alright?"

"I thought you said we weren't going to fight."

"I'm hoping it doesn't come down to that. And if anyone is fighting, it's me."

"I can fight."

"Can you avoid using your ability during said fight? One spark from you and this whole building goes up."

"I-"

"If you can't fight without help from your ability, then I'm sidelining you. I want this place gone, sure, but I won't have that happen with you or Pearl still in it."

"What about you?"

I didn't know what to say to him. I couldn't just say that I was not planning on making it out of there alive, he'd probably tell me that I had to. In the short amount of time that I've known him, I could tell he was one of the people that would be unwilling to leave me behind if I told him to, especially if he was going to blow up the building. So I couldn't tell him and risk him trying to stop me.

"I'm gonna try and get out, but you and her are my priorities."

I felt bad lying through my teeth, but I had to tell him what he wanted to hear — not that those words specifically were what he wanted to hear. I just couldn't let him know what my plan truly was. I couldn't put that on him to know.

"What are we going to do?"

"We need to get downstairs. I have a feeling that's where he'll be keeping Pearl."

"Do you think he's expecting you?"

"I would think so, why else would he give me her location?"

Seriously, if he was going to kill her, he would've done it by now. This had to be a trap. There's no way it wasn't.

Speak of the devil.

"Flint, keep going. Just stay vigilant. Come back if there is anything."

We almost seemed to have an unspoken understanding between us as he kept creeping around the second floor. Meanwhile, I had a phone call to take.

"Mr. Crane, what do I owe the pleasure?"

"I have your sister."

"You told me this already."

"And I'm going to kill her."

"You texted me that too. What else is new?"

"Do you not care? This is your sister."

Of course, I cared, but he didn't need to know that. He didn't need to know my plans or how much I was willing to do for her.

"Yeah, she's my sister, and you told me where to find her body. Is it done? Can I come get it?"

I could only imagine his mouth hanging open as I said that. I couldn't show my emotions or my deep connection to Pearl. I couldn't risk doing that.

Just focus on your plan. Don't get distracted by emotions. Emotions make you weak.

"You didn't want to come stop me? I gave you the address. You could come stop me."

"Why would I do that? You said you were going to kill her. How do I not know she isn't dead already and my coming there would result in the same fate for me?"

I hated how easily it came out of my mouth and how believable it sounded. I sounded like a selfish prick, only caring about my life. I swear I wanted to help my sister out. I swear I valued her life over mine.

"She's not dead yet. You could still save her?"

"Prove it!"

"It's for you, girl."

"It's your big brother."

"Speak, bitch!"

If I could reach through the phone and rip his tongue from his head, believe me, I would. Nobody speaks to my sister that way, and got to live after. Then again, he wasn't going to be alive in the next few hours — that I could promise. I just only wished I could kill him now and not have had to deal with this hassle.

"Sean?"

I could barely make my name out of her hoarse voice — it broke me. Even when I held Damien captive, I gave him water and food. Yeah, I tortured him on the side, but still, I wasn't a complete monster where I'd deprive him of necessities to survive.

"There! Now you have proof she's alive."

"Ha! Barely! She's dehydrated and sounds barely conscious. I wouldn't call that alive."

Cool it, Sean!

Don't let your emotions get the best of you. He can't hear your empathy. He can't know you care.

"You heard her voice. Besides, she doesn't need anything. She'll be dead soon, that is if you don't show."

"That's a bummer. I don't think I'll be able to make it there in time."

"What? What time would you be able to get here?"

"I'm not sure."

This was most definitely a trap.

"Why do you care so much, Crane? You already have her, what do you need with me?"

"I just want to meet the man who killed my son."

"Hate to break it to you, but that guy would have been one of the dead ones in the tunnel. Whichever guy blew the door up, that's your son's killer."

"Don't lie to me! Don't make excuses!"

"Why would I-"

"I know it was you! You merciless killer! You killed my son! My heir!"

Why did he have to start screaming? I had to pull the phone away from my ear to avoid damage — that's how annoyingly loud he was wailing.

"I may be a merciless killer, but your son's death wasn't done by my hand. I made his death easier by putting him out of his pain-"

Shit! That sounded bad.

That came out all wrong!

"You bastard! You killed my son!"

Yeah, I can't take back what I said, and there was no way he was going to change his mind. I should have chosen my words more carefully.

"Why don't you come here, so I can meet you face-to-face?"

"I'm not sure about that, sir. As I said, I'm a bit of a drive away. I won't make it there in time."

"I'll make sure you-"

"umm, boss?"

"What?"

"One of the guys says there's a car outside. It's parked about a mile out."

Shit!

I figured I parked far enough away and got enough coverage from some trees that they wouldn't see it. Unless they were doing perimeter checks.

"Okay and? It could be abandoned."

"Hey, boss?"

What is it now? How many men did he have needing his attention right now?

"Is there anyone supposed to be doing a round on the second floor?"

Almost on cue, Flint flew around the corner, sprinting directly at me.

"Nobody should be doing rounds upstairs!"

"Who would-"

"It's you, isn't it?"

I barely registered what he said. I figured he was still talking to his henchmen. Plus, Flint was trying to mouth words to me.

"Ah frowned your."

What?

"dude, what?"

"A flounder."

"I don't understand you."

"A"

"Round?"

No. *Bound?*

"Ear?"

What does that even mean?

Aren't all ears rounded?

But he could have said bound ear? What the fuck does that mean? A bound ear?

So, I might be bad a reading lips.

"Sean Barnes?"

"Yeah!"

Oh shit!

I was still on the phone with Mr. Crane.

"Are you there?"

"Yup, just got distracted by some waitress."

"Really?"

"Uh-huh. She's got these big ti- eyes. Bright blue."

"That's interesting."

"I thought so too."

"Do you know why your vehicle would be out here then? You left your registration in the car."

"My car?"

"Yeah, your car."

"Oh! That was stolen several weeks ago. I haven't seen it in a few days. Where is it?"

"What about the person upstairs?"

"Upstairs? I'm confused."

"Are you in my building, Sean Barnes?"

"What? No! I told you where I was."

"Sean, I know a liar when I hear one. Why don't you come down here, and we can talk properly?"

Do I give up the lie? Do I keep going?

I mean, if I do give up, he only thinks it's me up here. That could be the perfect distraction for Flint to grab Pearl and get out. Then again, if I keep playing dumb, I could get his men to come up here, and I could easily take them out — but that would mean risking Flint. He couldn't be caught. Crane couldn't know he was here too.

"Fine, I'll come down. But make sure those guns are holstered, or else it won't be a pretty sight."

"You have my word. I'll even have some men meet you at the stairs."

I didn't trust his word. It was worth shit. He said he was going to kill Pearl, and she was still alive — though I'm grateful she still was. Still, there was no trusting this man, but I didn't have a choice anymore. I had to be a distraction. Flint had to get Pearl and get out.

"It'll be a party then. See you in a sec."

Of course, I had to get the last words in. Though I'm sure he tried to say something before I rudely hung up on him. I didn't really care what he had to say. I was more interested in what Flint was trying to say.

"I found her, dumbass."

Oh!

That makes more sense.

"Why did you give yourself up?"

"Because I'm trying to give you two a chance at getting out."

"But what if they look back at her when you distract them? They'll see me."

"Trust me, I know how to keep men like Crane distracted. It's a technique I learned long ago. It's called, piss them right off and hope they attack."

"That doesn't sound like a good plan."

"It's not, but it makes for a good distraction."

"What do I do when I get her and get out?"

"Well, you'll need to rehydrate her when you get to her — I'll give you my bag so you have everything. As soon as you are both cleared from the building, get the sparks going."

"But you'll be inside?"

"Don't worry about me. I'll make it back to you guys."

I'm glad he couldn't tell when I was lying, this would make the conversation very difficult.

"You promise you won't leave me?"

"What?"

"You promise you'll get out?"

"Yeah, I'll get out."

"Promise?"

Fuck!

"I promise I'll get out, Flint. For you and Pearl, I'll get out."

But if I happened to get trapped in, I wouldn't have to break my promise — technically. I could try and get out, but ultimately my path would be blocked. Then my promise wouldn't be broken.

"We need you. She needs her big brother, and I need support."

"You have Pearl to support you."

"But there's only so much she understands. You're older. You have more experience and knowledge than her."

"Don't let her hear you say that. She'll kick your ass."

"I know. Just promise me you'll get out."

"Kiddo, I promise."

"Now, let's go kick some ass."

Well, let me go kick some ass. Flint's getting Pearl and getting the hell out of here.

"Be smart."

I was not entirely sure if I was talking to Flint or myself, but still I had to say it. We both needed to hear it.

Now, the fun part, meeting the devil himself and barely being able to breathe because Flint has the oxygen, plus dealing with some amateur henchmen — I don't know about you, but definitely sounds like a party.

At least he was true to his word about the men waiting for me by the stairs. They didn't even attempt to go up to them, but probably because they didn't trust me. Mr. Crane didn't trust me. But I couldn't blame them, I barely trusted myself sometimes. Since Crane kept to his word, his men didn't see me motion for Flint to go down a different set of stairs, nor did they see Flint in general. I'm not sure if Crane telling them to wait for me at the stairwell was the best or worst idea. On one hand, it would mean avoiding being in direct and confined spaces with me, where I'd easily incapacitate them. Meanwhile, on the other, I could not have been alone — which I wasn't — and they would never know because they didn't come upstairs to see. His logic could go both ways in being smart or idiotic.

"You guys come here often?"

Sue me for trying to converse with the henchmen. Sure, they were trying to seem intimidating — failing miserably — but let's be honest, they weren't the scariest men I've encountered.

"I couldn't imagine why you would, it smells horrible out here. It's almost like a robot hybrid died in here somewhere and is rotting."

Still silence.

Rude.

"I don't know how any of you are breathing this air in so casually. I feel like I'm going to puke."

"What's that thing?"

Whoa! One of them speaks! I figured they weren't allowed to talk to me.

"What's what thing?"

"A robot hybrid."

They both could speak! Look at us go, making process.

"You don't know what that is."

I stopped in my tracks. There was no way they didn't know what that was. Everyone with even a bit of money or social media knew what they were.

"No, we don't know."

How did they seriously not know? Did Crane make them live under a rock when they didn't work?

"I mean it's in the name. Robot hybrid. Like people who are bionically altered."

"People do that?"

"All the time, especially for medical issues. People replace muscles, tissue, bones, and anything you can think of, with robotic parts. You didn't know?"

"Why would they do that?"

"It's one of the ways doctors cure arthritis, replacing those joints with robotic joints. It's standard procedure now."

"So people are becoming Cyclops?"

"That's a being with one eye, so no."

"Stupid! They're called cyborgs."

"Hey!"

I was not expecting the one to smack the other on the side of the head.

"Most people don't really prefer that term. They're just people who have been genetically altered for their health. Then again, some people do it for fun."

"Why would anyone do that for fun?"

Anyone with money would gladly alter their bodies to be better. If only they knew the consequences of being born different. It was stupid! Society hated anyone born different — born with an ability of some sort — yet here, these people were willingly altering themselves to be different. How did that make any sense? How was that fair? If only those in Normalis could see those people now. Maybe then they'd turn on their own kind? Wishful thinking.

"Many professional athletes do it. With a robotic arm, you could triple your distance in throwing a ball. With a robotic leg, you could achieve so much — kicking the winning goal, running the fastest, you name it. People want to be known for their achievements, they don't care how they get it."

"You're telling me that athletes do that?"

"Yeah! Most of them are phoneys and cheaters."

"How are they cheating?" "I don't believe you."

I almost didn't catch either of them. Why did they have to talk over each other?

"They are cheaters because they lie on their contracts stating they have no alterations in their bodies. They are supposed to disclose that before being signed onto a team. Most don't, therefore, they are cheaters."

"How do you know this?" "Whoa!"

Seriously! They need to stop that!

"I watch sports. I follow which athletes are succeeding in their sports and try to support those who aren't cheating assholes."

"Are they all like that?" "The world is so cool. I want to be like that."

"You guys need to talk one at a time!"

"Are they all-?" "The world is so cool. I want to be like that."

"Stupid, let me talk first!"

"Are they all like that?"

"No, not all of them. But most are. People with money tend to do the stupidest things with their money. If I'm being honest, I'm surprised none of you are bionic."

"Wait! You think we are like that?"

"I want to be like that. I want to be a Cyclops."

"Cyborg, stupid!"

"Right! I want to be a cyborg!"

"Why do you think we're like that?"

"Because you'd be able to do things more effectively. Why else?"

"I want that!"

"Shut up!"

"How would we do things more effectively?"

"Depends on the modification. You could protect your boss easier with a robotic torso, or could be stronger with robotic legs and arms."

"You think?"

"Shut up, stupid!"

"But what he said. Do you think we could be better?"

"Yeah. So many people do it to be better and more powerful."

"Is that what you and your sister did?"

"Yeah, is that what you guys did?"

"What?"

"Didn't you and your sister do that? I mean, I was there when she killed Roger. Punched a hole right through him as if he wasn't made of flesh and bone."

"So, did you and your sister become cyborgs?"

Would it be wrong to laugh in this guy's face? It's not his fault he's been sheltered from what happens in society. But still, really? Did Crane not tell his men anything? How much were they left in the dark?

"No. I'm not a cyborg."

"But you're something."

"Yeah. I'm a walking weapon. Something that people can't detect when going into important places. My sister is too. You're just lucky you caught her at a bad time."

Flint was right about my twisted nature. I had to hide my smile as both men took a step away from me. I'm glad they were scared of me.

"Oh."

Cute. I've made them speechless.

"C'mon boys, let's get going. Can't keep the boss waiting any longer, now can we."

From all the things I heard about Mr. Crane and the things he had done, I imagined him to be a powerful-looking man, dressed in a suit and looking like he meant business. Maybe throw in a few tattoos and that was the man I imagined. Honestly, the idea that I created of him in my head was almost scary. I expected to walk into the room and find a scary-looking buff dude with his sleeves rolled up exposing tattoos. Obviously, I let my mind run wild with that image. What I didn't expect to find was a totally different man.

I wouldn't say that this man was short, maybe about an average size, but he was definitely shorter than I was — I had at least five inches over him. He did sport somewhat of a fancy suit just as I thought, yet the physique that I was imagining did not match. This man looked about one beer away from popping the button. I should probably feel bad for thinking of such a thing, but it made it difficult given that behind him my sister was tied to a chair. Plus he had just called her a bitch. I didn't feel bad after that. He was a fat man who deserved the slandering in my mind. Though I would be nice and keep my cruel comments inside, I didn't want to risk getting Pearl hurt by insulting this man.

"Hey, boss. Here he is."

"Sean Barnes, what a-"

"Hey, boss? I got a question."

"Not the time, stupid!"

"I need to ask it before I forget."

"He's busy! It can wait!"

"I'm not busy now since I was so rudely interrupted."

Maybe I didn't need to distract them. Perhaps they'd distract themselves and this would be an easier task for me.

"Ask your stupid question before I shoot you!"

"Right! Thank you, boss!"

"We were discussing why you never made us into cyclops-"

"Cyborgs."

"Yeah, why did you never let us become those."

"What are you two on about?"

"We just want to be better for you." "We want to be robotic!"

"One at a time fools."

"Hey, you seem really busy. Maybe we should do this another time?"

"You're not going anywhere."

Okay, so Mr. Crane has a gun on him. Maybe he was starting to fit that image in my mind.

"Whoa! No need for the auxiliary."

"Stay there."

I'm staying here.

That gun was going to make a few things messy now. If Crane even caught a whiff of our plan, he'd end everything right now. If he saw Flint, the chances were high that the arsonist would get a bullet to the head. How was I going to go about this? How was I going to protect both of those kids?

"We're just saying that if we were to get robotic parts, we could be better workers for you."

"Are you listening to yourselves? We get rid of those who are different! We don't become like them!"

"But boss, it would be beneficial for you."

"No, it wouldn't! It would defeat the whole purpose of our mission!"

"Boss-"

"Stop talking!"

"You!"

ME?!

"How can I help you?"

"You put these pathetic ideas into their heads!"

"I would never."

"How else would they come up with such an idiotic idea?"

"I think it's pretty obvious where they got this idea. I mean, look at them. They're not very smart."

I'm not sure why I felt like acting this way. Maybe because it was entertaining to make the short man mad? Perhaps I was just tired of being serious.

Oh.

I've been inhaling too much of this gas.

Was I fucking high?

"We just think-"

"I told you to stop talking! You're done talking now! Go do something useful before I kill you for being so dumb!"

"Boss-"

"Shut up!"

"Get out!"

That was rude. They were just trying to be better men for the company. Why was he such a bitter small man?

I'm high. Fuck!

"Where was I?"

"'Sean Barnes, what a—'. That's where you were."

"Thank you?"

I needed to get some proper oxygen. This is not who I was as a person — well, not when I was on an assignment. I could be high on my own time, just not right now.

"Any chance you could crack a window or let me get some air? This smell is giving me a wicked headache."

Ew. I hated how airy I sounded. I really needed some oxygen.

"I can't think properly when I have a headache."

At least Crane wasn't an asshole about this, probably because he wanted me to be coherent with whatever he wanted to tell me.

Spoke too soon. Of course, he had to jump right back into being an asshole as he put his gun up to my temple. Did he think I was going to do anything? I was fucking loopy. How did he not see that? Maybe I should be glad he didn't see my shift in cognition.

"Keep an eye on the girl. We'll be right back."

She was tied up — not for long. Where was she supposed to go?

Even I knew that was bullshit. Even if she was tied up, she could easily get out of the chair. Okay, makes sense why Mr. Crane would want someone to keep an eye on her.

Hopefully, Flint could deal with the one guy if they saw him.

How's that for a distraction? Get the bad guy away from my sister!

I'm smart! See!

Even slightly incoherent I was able to follow and execute the plan.

"So, whatcha want to talk about about?"

"I want you dead."

"Join the party."

"But I won't kill you."

No shocker there.

"I know. You're going to sell us back to my mother and hopefully get a grand reward for doing so."

"You're smart, but there's something you're missing."

What could I be missing? She wanted us and he was planning on selling us back to her. What else could there be?

"What am I missing?"

His laugh was just as bone-chilling and just as annoying as his son's. Now I could see where Damien got from.

"She only wants one of you. She wants you to fight. Whichever wins goes back to her, and the other dies in the fight, or we'll take care of them."

"That's not happening."

"Excuse — you have no choice in the matter!"

"I'm pretty sure I do."

"No, you don't! If you don't fight then I'll kill you and send your little sister there myself!"

"And what if my sister isn't the strongest? You know they won't take it lightly if you gave them the dud and killed the other."

I didn't know which one of us was stronger. I was honestly asking a hypothetical question while trying to threaten him.

"That's why you'll be fighting."

"I won't fight my sister."

My job was to protect her. Not hurt or kill her. I wouldn't fight my sister, even if it meant staying alive longer.

"She said the same thing."

Is it strange that I was relieved to hear that? I mean, I always thought she resented me for leaving her behind. But hearing that she spoke about me to Flint in a positive matter and rejected Crane's suggestion warmed my heart. I didn't deserve her as a sister. Pearl was too innocent and compassionate for her own good.

I truly didn't deserve to have her support or love.

I was and will always be a killer. Killers didn't deserve that kind of person in their life. They didn't deserve that kind of light in their darkness.

"Then there will be no fight."

"There will be! I said so!" He snapped. I'm surprised he didn't stomp his foot at that moment.

"Are you a kid? Stop throwing a tantrum!"

"Why you-"

He was uncoordinated and slow. Or maybe it was just that I was better and coming out of that fog? Obviously, I was better — I was trained to be the best of the best and to anticipate movements. I knew what he was going to do the second I felt the gun move away from my head. He was trying to hit me with it. That or he was planning on killing me now. Either way, I was faster than him. I grabbed his arm before he could do anything.

"Wha-"

"Did you think that would work?"

"I said I wouldn't fight my sister, I said nothing about fighting you. I'd gladly knock you the fuck out."

"Why ah-"

I didn't even punch him that hard. Just gave him a little bop on the nose, nothing he didn't deserve. That bop pushed him a few feet from me and left me with the gun. He didn't intentionally leave the gun, but with me holding his arm, he didn't have much of a choice. Now I had the gun pointed at him.

I didn't entirely know how this model worked, but I could figure it out quickly. He was now at my mercy, even if it didn't feel that way. I felt like I was missing something. I had to be missing something. There was no way he could be this calm during the situation.

"Here's how this going to go. We're going back inside, you're going to call off your men and then Pearl and I are walking out of here."

"I don't think that's how that will go. You'd have to kill me if you want to walk out of here."

"Don't tempt me!"

I hated how calm he was. A normal person would have reacted to my aggressive tone. His son would have reacted in fear. Why wasn't he? How was he remaining so calm? What was I missing?

"Do you really think by killing me, you'll survive? Do you think your sister will survive?"

"Do you think your men will survive if I kill you right now?"

I had to counteract his words. He was trying to threaten me — trying to remain in control of the situation. I couldn't let him do that. He wasn't the one in control, he never was. I had planned for this. Flint and I had planned this out logically, Crane was never in control of this.

"Do you really need more blood on your hands? Don't you want it to be just one?"

"That one being my sister's?"

"Exactly!"

Ha! Was he insane? Did he think his suggestion would sway my plan? He couldn't be serious.

"I would rather have all the blood from the world on my hands if it meant my sister was alive and healthy."

"So much for not caring for her. Not caring if she was dead or not."

Fuck!

Don't show vulnerability! That was the one thing I wasn't allowed to have. I wasn't supposed to show it.

People could not know my vulnerability.

Pearl.

Pearl was mine. She was everything to me. She was my future and my life.

Pearl deserved everything in the world.

"I'm allowed to care for my sister."

"But you more than care about her. You'd do anything for her. You love her."

"Sue me for loving my little sister! You act like it's a crime to do so. Do you not love your children?"

"My son is dead because of you!"

"You still have a daughter. And Damien's death wasn't on me! Your men blew up the door and the shrapnel killed him. That wasn't my fault!"

"You kidnapped him!"

"He was going to do the same to me! I just acted quicker!"

How was this being turned on me? I did exactly what Damien was going to do with me. Why was he losing his shit on me? It wasn't my fault!

"Don't hate me because I was just better than your son! He's the one who fucked up his mission and I took control of the situation. Just like I'm going to do now!"

"My son was innocent. He was human!"

Of course, that's his response — because being human means being exempt from things. How was that fair? Damien tried to kidnap me, wanted to torture me, and yet when I did that to him, I was in the wrong. Why? Because I wasn't entirely human.

"I didn't ask to be what I am!"

I never asked to be created in a lab!

I never asked to be superhuman!

I never asked to be born!

"Don't turn this on me! Your son was just shitty at his job, and he paid the price! Now it's your turn."

"My turn?"

"Your turn to pay the price for fucking with us! You don't fuck with the Barnes' and get away with it!"

"And you definitely don't get away with calling one of them a bitch!"

"You deserved it! You all deserve to die! You're unnatural!"

"No! We're supernatural and we're probably the most normal and natural things there are."

"I'm human! I'm natural!"

"Please! Your kind is as natural as a steel light post!"

I wasn't technically wrong. With the number of robotic parts people modify for themselves, they have more metal than flesh and bone.

"We never chose to be different! None of us ever asked to be this way! But you humans, you all chose to be different and don't face the consequences of it. You're more of the monsters than any of us!"

"I don't know what you are talking about!"

"You! Your kind! You're all the same. You sell people for money and influence. You think you're helping the world by getting rid of supernaturals, but you're just enabling psychos to create more. The government wants power and so they use people like me to get rid of competition. Anyone with money wants to be powerful and different, so they modify themselves to be that way. All you humans are the same!"

"I don't-"

"That's right, you don't know anything!"

"I-"

"Shut your fucking mouth!"

I finally broke him. Why did it feel so satisfying? Why was it so gratifying watching him crumple to his knees? Why did I like seeing him beg?

"Please? I don't deserve this." He pleads, falling to the ground.

"You don't? Then who does?"

"Not me! I'm innocent!"

God, he was trying to make me laugh. Of course, he deserved this.

"Get up, coward!"

Scrambling to his feet, I dragged him back into the building. I wanted his men to see his fragility. They deserved to see the kind of man they followed.

"Look at you now, Mr. Crane!"

"A coward!"

"A fraud!"

"A nobody!"

"Pathetic!"

"A pathetic waste of air!"

"Boss?"

"Shut up! I'm speaking!"

"Tell them what you begged from me!"

They had to see the kind of man Mr. Crane was. It was only fair.

"I don't deserve to die. I'm innocent in all of this. These men here were the ones who did everything! They kidnapped the creatures! They are the ones who shipped them to be sold! They're the ones who took your sister!"

"Under whose order?"

"Don't make me repeat myself!"

"Mine-"

"Speak up!" How dare he speak so quiet in a moment like this?

"It was my order!"

"Good. Glad you confirmed."

I'll save you from the gory details: but let's just say as his body fell to the ground it had two arms and a head less. And as promised, his head was also missing a tongue. He couldn't get away with calling my sister a bitch, and he didn't deserve to scream as I mangled him.

"Now gentlemen, if you want to walk away from this, I suggest you go now. You won't like what happens next if you don't leave."

I looked around at the terrified faces of his men. It was almost like they were too scared to move. "No?"

"Nobody wants to leave?"

"Alright then, I warned you."

I did warn them. I blame their lack of response on the shock of watching their boss being beheaded, but I gave them a choice. Nobody took the opportunity. They now would suffer the same fate as their boss.

"Had you guys done your job properly, you would have noticed that you are a person short."

"Now, before you look around at each other wondering who was missing. If you turn your gaze over to the left, please notice the empty chair."

"You know, the person you were supposed to be watching? Yeah! She's gone."

Surprise!

Now that's what I call a distraction!

"You should have taken your jobs more seriously, then maybe you wouldn't have lost your leverage."

"That doesn't matter anymore. I enjoyed the chat we had earlier, you two." I motioned to the two idiots who I met intially. "I just wish we weren't on opposite sides, I would have kept you two alive if that was the case."

"But as all good things go, they must come to an end."

"It was nice to meet you all."

"What are you going to do?"

"Oh! I'm not doing anything! I'm waiting just like you are."

"But I think it's time to speed up the process."

"Flint! Go ahead!" I called out.

"Flint?" "Who's that?"

I had to hand it to the kid I hadn't been expecting him to actually follow through with our plan of blowing up the building. I figured I would've had to pester these guys to the point where one of them wanted to shoot me or something, and then I could use the sparks from the bullet ricocheting off of whatever to start the fire — I swear I had a backup plan just in case this kid didn't work out. Thankfully though, he followed through, and all I had to do was bask in the impending flame that would be my demise.

I was ready.

But if you didn't know this already, I survived. Instead of being torched to death like everyone else in the room, I had a bubble formed around me. That fucking kid was holding out on me. He was in more control than I originally thought. And he read through my promise like it was nothing, knowing damn well I wouldn't follow through or have some excuse to not follow through — like being trapped in the fire.

"Were you going to tell me that you could create a gap in the fire to protect someone?"

Lo and behold, there was a little shit and my sister standing outside waiting for me to come out of the blazing building.

"Were you going to tell me you planned on using it to end your life?"

"Touché."

Maybe the kid wasn't so bad after all. I guess I can get used to him.

"Are you kidding me? You planned on saving me and then getting yourself killed? Where is the logic in that?"

"When you put it like that, it makes me sound like an asshole, P."

"You are an asshole!"

Ouch! So much for her praising me and caring about me still.

"I'm a killer, what do you expect me to-"

"Stop using that excuse! You're more than just a killer, you know it and I know it." Leave it to my sister to argue with me.

"I don't think I do know that."

"Of course you do. If you truly were a killer you wouldn't be here right now you'd be trying to make a paycheque by murdering someone. You'd put yourself back in the program if you were one. But you didn't and you're here, so that means you're more than just a killer."

"Stop it! You're supposed to hate me. I left remember!" I snapped.

"I know you did, but I can't hate you. I know why you did it, but I wish you had asked me my opinion before you did it."

"Why? So you could have yelled at me for being a horrible brother for trying to leave?"

"No, asshole! So I could tell you that the only way I'd have a better life was if you were in it."

"Awe."

"Shut it, Finley!"

Sean, don't you dare start crying. They'll never let you live it down if you do. Did I really want to be bullied by these two?

Hold it together, man!

"I'm sorry I left." I was quiet. What if she didn't hear me? Would I be able to repeat myself?

"I'm sorry you left too." She smirked.

"Can you forgive me?"

Why was she thinking about that? Why did she have to think so hard about that? I thought she forgave me already. She said she understood why I left, didn't that mean she forgave me?

"Of course, I forgive you. I want my asshole, big brother back in my life." Hearing her admit made my heart slam against my rib cage.

Don't you fucking dare start watering, eyes!

"I want to be back in your life too."

"Then come back. Let's be the siblings we used to be." Her voice soft, but full of warmth.

"Will you accept me back?"

"Yes, now get over here and give me a hug."

"Group hug?" Flint suggested.

"Fine! You get in here too, Finley."

Cliché I know, but we hugged it out. And then went back to the diner where I made Flint pay for our meal, and we lived happily ever after.

The end.

I'm just kidding, that's not how it went.

"Hey Flint, how do you feel about blowing something else up?"

"Well, you're kind of my ride back into the city, so I'm down to do whatever."

"Good!"

"What are you thinking, Sean?"

"I think there should be a new building put up near my place, and it's going to need a demolition crew with a lot of firepower to take it down. You guys in?"

"I'm so in!"

"Do I even have a choice?"

"Nope!"

Flint and I knew each other so well. We were even thinking the same things. It's crazy how quickly someone can become an important part of your life.

"Let's go then."

"I call shotgun!"

"I'll grab a shotgun if you take the front seat, Finley." Leave it to my sister to make a threat so casually.

"I call the back seat!"

"That's what I thought."

Oh, we were a hundred percent siblings.

Burn the building down — or maybe it's the whole block that was being burnt down.

Watch as the skyscraper's windows are blown out — there isn't any chance those will be replaced anytime soon.

Relish in the heat on the face. The bitter taste of smoke and metal lingered in the air — yet it wasn't the worst taste there was. It almost tasted rewarding. Not only saving my sister but another person I said I'd help. This fire was my reward.

The crackle of the hardwood foyer was music to my ears. The flames danced across the floor as if partners in a language that they only knew.

Burn it all down. Crane's hard work and legacy burnt to a crisp.

I'd say it was a satisfying end to the story.

Crane really shouldn't have messed with those whom he didn't understand. Especially shouldn't have fought fire with an arsonist. Who did he think would win?

Then again, he never did fight. He cowarded like the bitch he was and expected his men to do the damage. They didn't know how to properly inflict damage and were never properly trained. It showed.

In the end, he got what he deserved. They all did.

They shouldn't have started a fight with someone that was designed to kill — they'd end up dead. They shouldn't have started a business based on hurting people — they'd reap what they sowed.

Somebody should have warned the man before he based the last few hours and years on this business. It wasn't a fair fight, and he should have known.

Poor guy.

All his hard work was reduced to nothingness. Crane was reduced to nothingness.

It's sad. But he deserved it.

You don't fight fire with gas!

You don't fight ex-assassins with amateurs!

You don't kidnap supernaturals and expect them to take the assault lightly!

You don't fight with people much stronger than you!

Just don't start the fight.

But if you do?

Expect those who you disrespected to be standing watching your empire burn. They'll just end up roasting marshmallows over your downfall and walking away with minor injuries.

Don't start the fight!

Don't fuck with those you don't understand!

And don't forget to read the fine print!

Don't fuck with the Barnes',
Don't fuck with supernaturals,
They'll end up being your demise.

EPILOGUE

The black-bound book found itself shut and placed gently into the lap of the long-haired woman. Gently, she traced the faded words on the cover— Deadly Allegiance: Sean Barnes' Story was etched in. It was almost astonishing that even through countless centuries, this book was still legible and only contained a few imperfections. Despite the numerous times it had been opened, the spine was still intact, minus the obvious line down the middle. Sean's red name, along with the darkness of the black color, was beginning to fade from the front, and the top right corner of the book was bent but otherwise, the book was in near-perfect condition. It astonished the young lady at how far it had traveled and still looked the way it did. They needed to keep it that way as well. She carefully brought it back to its specific spot on the bookshelf.

A gentle smile graced her face as she saw the spine and could make out the folded words underneath the title: 'Did I say you could read this?' remembering the first time she noticed those words. Only Sean would come up with some phrase to deter people from looking into his story. But it never stopped her, and she didn't want it to prevent her son either. There is a lot he could still learn from Sean.

"That's it?" the young boy asked from his propped-up pillow.

"What do you mean, monkey?" she replied, settling back down at the foot of his bed.

"Is that seriously all you're going to read me? Where's the rest? I mean, what happened to the gore? What happened to the excitement? What happened to the information Waverly gave him? What about Heather Crane, where did she end up?" Despite his young age, the young boy was already accustomed to the brutality and horrors of the world.

"You know how the story ends. They did what they could with that information Waverly gave and went after the rest of the company. And the same thing happened with Heather Crane, they went after her."

"Seriously? That's not what I was expecting! I wanted more gore! I wanted to watch all the bad guys pay for their crimes!"

"Why would you want that?"

"Why wouldn't I? He detailed his torture of that other guy, and yet he opted out of telling the brutality of murdering the rest, especially Mr. Crane. Why? I want to know. It's not fair!"

She gave a patient smile. "I think his conscious decision to avoid talking about the death of Mr. Crane shows his development. He doesn't want to be seen by just his actions."

"That's dumb and boring. Why would you read that entry to me?"

"Monkey, you know that not all the stories can be overly entertaining. But if you were listening closely, you'd see there was a lesson to be learned."

She often said that lessons lived within the journals. She's learned many herself, and now she hoped her son would, too.

"What's the lesson? That humans suck. Mom, I knew how shitty humans were."

"Watch your language, monkey."

"You swear all the time."

"I'm your mother, I'm allowed to. Now tell me what's the real lesson learned and not the obvious one."

"Other than the fact that this guy is boring, and I would've preferred to hear about anyone else. Well, I would've preferred to hear about our direct ancestry."

"I've told you you're not ready yet."

"I know, but I still would've preferred it."

"What's the lesson learned?"

"I don't know Mom, that this guy didn't know how to properly tell a story."

"Be serious."

"I am. I don't know what the lesson is, will you tell me?"

"Just this once, but the next one, you'll have to figure out yourself. You cannot rely on me all the time to give you all the answers."

"Fine. What's the lesson?"

"If you're paying enough attention, you would see that even if you're born to be a specific something, does not make you that thing for the rest of your life. Sean was born to be a killer, but it didn't mean he had to be one for the rest of his life."

"And yet he still killed those men."

"Monkey, that was only a snippet of his life. Had I read you the rest of it, you'd see he didn't always resort to that action."

"So why didn't you read me more?"

"I thought you said he was boring and you needed more action"

"He is boring. I just wanna know why you only read this part."

She chuckled softly. "I told you this before, the journal entries I read are supposed to help you learn something. Their lives are more than just these journals. They've done so much more with them, but as of right now, I think you can benefit from only hearing a few entries."

"Fine. But why are you reading these people? Why not just read from our direct ancestors? Their journals are right here. Why not just read them?"

"Monkey, you need to see who our family was from a different perspective before delving into their own minds and stories. You need an outside perspective before you can see the inner turmoil."

"It's not fair. Why can't I learn our history? Hear our history? That would be much more entertaining."

"I'm sure it would, but then your opinions would be muddled. You'd only see our family from one side of the story, not from any other. If you're going to learn anything about this world, you will need to look at both sides before you can make conclusions."

"That's annoying!"

"You'll get over it. You will need to learn to open your mind to both sides of the coin."

"What does that mean?"

"It's just an old saying, meaning you need to have an open mind for different perspectives of the world."

"Well, it's dumb, and not fair."

"Monkey-"

"I'm not talking to you anymore."

It was in moments like these that the woman recognized that her son was still young. She was almost joyous that he had these moments— these tantrums— showing that he was not fully corrupted by the world. He still had his childlike nature.

"Would you feel better if you chose the next journal?"

Her son tried to hide his excitement, only to fail miserably as he jumped from the bed.

"Can I?"

"Go ahead but remember you cannot choose from THAT shelf. I won't read you any story from our direct ancestors just yet."

"Fine!"

He scurried over to the bookshelf, running his finger along the spines. He had to pick the perfect one for the next night. But he wanted to be clever about his pick. His mother said he couldn't choose a direct ancestor's journal, yet she said nothing about their siblings' books. Excitedly, his finger stopped on a familiar book that he had seen on his mother's nightstand numerous times. Unlike Sean's journal, this one was much more aged and used. It's purple color, and golden letters faded to the point that the title's etching was the only thing that would let you know whose story you were about to read.

"I've got it!"

"Let's see?"

"A good choice, but-"

"But nothing, they technically aren't from our direct ancestry. And I think I can learn a lot from seeing this perspective of the family."

He had got her there. He was becoming clever and witty the more he aged.

"Okay, you win."

"Yes! And I think this journal will be much more interesting than the other guy."

"You know his name, monkey. Don't be disrespectful."

"I'm sorry. This next journal will be much more interesting than Sean Barnes'."

"We shall see."

"Okay, time to rest." she pulled the thick covers back. And let him scramble back into bed, where she tucked him tightly in. She didn't want him to fall or move out of bed like he had done before. The only way to do that was to make sure he was tightly tucked.

"Good night, my monkey."

She gently moved the journal onto the side table next to the glowing light. Under the light, it had a changing effect as the dark purple cover glowed like a pastel. What was left of the gold lettering also seemed to shimmer in the light.

"We'll pick this one up tomorrow."

Acknowledgements

I've been incredibly blessed to receive an overwhelming amount of support from family and friends as I embark on this journey of storytelling, specifically with my debut novel *Deadly Allegiance*. From this support there are a few extraordinary people who have been crucial in helping me reach the point of completing this novel, and I want to take a moment to express my deepest gratitude to them.

First, I want to start with my parents.

To Mom, your wisdom and guidance on the logistical side of writing and publishing my book has been priceless information. I know it wasn't easy to be the one to slow me down, especially when I was eager to rush into publishing with the first company I found. But I'm glad you did. With your careful research and connections to people going on a similar journey, you have given me unwavering support, and thoughtful advice – which is everything I needed. I'll never forget the after-dinner conversations with you, Mom, where you patiently talked me through the publishing process – even if at the time it seemed like I wasn't listening. You always knew how to ground me when I felt overwhelmed. I am forever grateful for your steady hand guiding me through this process.

To Dad, your boundless optimism and endless encouragement have been a lifeline to me. Your willingness to read through my raw, unpolished drafts, even when it was hard, showed me just how much you believe in me. You've been my rock, my number one fan, shining a light on my path through the darkest of times. Not that I let it show, but the times I felt like giving up on my dream, your belief in me,

Dad, made me realize that I wasn't alone in my struggles. Your constant encouragement kept me pushing forward. Both you and Mom have nurtured my creativity with so much love, and without that, this book would never have been written. Thank you from the bottom of my heart for believing in me every step of the way.

To my sister, Victoria, words can't fully express how much your love and encouragement have meant throughout this process. You've listened to my endless ramblings, never once doubting my dreams, even when I was tangled in my own thoughts. You've been my sounding board and my biggest cheerleader, and for that, I am beyond thankful. I am so grateful for everything you've done to help me bring this book to life – even if you are still confused on what is happening.

To my dear friend Brandi, your patience and dedication to my storytelling have been a gift I'll always treasure. You've been there through years of twists, turns, and countless plot ideas, and your willingness to listen and collaborate on how to make this book—and future ones—truly shine means the world to me. I know my late-night writing sessions and constant brainstorming sessions were tough to keep up with, Brandi, but your support has never faltered. I am so thankful for your patience. You are a rare friend, and I am so lucky to have you by my side.

To my darling friend Noelle, your constructive and thought-out feedback has been a crucial part of this journey. You've never been afraid to give me the tough love I needed, and it's always been perfectly timed – especially now as I finish reading the revisions. You know exactly what to say and when to say it. Your insights have shaped this book into something I'm so proud of. I couldn't have made it this far without your honest and thoughtful input.

To my romance book loving friend Mandy, I try to not hold it against you that you love the romance genre over the fantasy genre. But other than that, I have to say I'll never be able to thank you enough for your advice on publishing. Your encouragement and belief in me pushed me to keep going when I wasn't sure I could. Reaching this point feels surreal, and I'm so grateful for you helping me get here. Hey Mandy, look I did it!

To my bunk bestie Erika, your consistent support has meant more to me than words can say. From the very beginning your encouragement and thoughtful advice has been a constant source of strength helping me continually improve – especially as I try to promote my book on Instagram and Tiktok. There are times when I really wish you could just be my manager, but for now, I'll gratefully take every nugget of wisdom you share with me. I'll continue to treasure your advice as I work to reach more followers. Thank you for being the push I need even when it feels like a struggle.

To my incredible work bestie Brook, even though you're a proud comic nerd (and I'll never let you forget it), I know I can always count on you to be there for me—especially when I need someone to talk through my chaotic thoughts. You've never once been thrown off by my weirdly morbid questions or my incessant need for your thoughts on certain scenes. Your insights have shaped the world I'm trying to build in ways I could never have imagined on my own. I truly can't thank you enough for being there as I stumble through the mess of publishing this book. Your unconditional support, your patience, and your ability to put up with me mean more to me than words can say. I'm beyond grateful to have you in my corner.

To my book coach, Mary, and my editor, Kerri, your expertise has turned my dreams into reality. The way you've helped me refine and shape this book has been beyond anything I could have hoped for. I am so thankful for everything you've done to help me get this far. I can't express enough how deeply appreciative I am of both of you.

To my entire circle of friends and family who have been there to cheer me on, offer a listening ear, and give me a reality check when I needed it—thank you. You are my heart and soul, and I couldn't have done this without each of you. My heart overflows with gratitude. Your love, support, and belief in me have been the foundation of this journey, and I will never be able to thank you enough for everything you've done. You've all made this experience unforgettable, and I am forever thankful to have you by my side. This book is as much yours as it is mine. I shall continue carrying each of you with me in every page, and I can't wait to see where this next chapter of my writing journey takes us.

As I turn the page to *Striking Midnight*, I know you'll continue to be there, cheering me on and helping me grow. Thank you for everything, from the bottom of my heart. Your support means everything to me.

Striking Midnight is coming soon!